Also by Claudia Mills

Write This Down

CLAUDIA MILLS

SQUARE
FISH

MARGARET FERGUSON BOOKS

Farrar Straus Giroux
New York

SQUARE
FISH

An imprint of Macmillan Publishing Group, LLC
175 Fifth Avenue
New York, NY 10010
mackids.com

WRITE THIS DOWN. Copyright © 2016 by Claudia Mills.
All rights reserved. Printed in the United States of America by
LSC Communications, Harrisonburg, Virginia

Square Fish and the Square Fish logo are trademarks of Macmillan and are used by
Farrar Straus Giroux under license from Macmillan.

Our books may be purchased in bulk for promotional, educational, or business use.
Please contact your local bookseller or the Macmillan Corporate and Premium
Sales Department at (800) 221-7945 ext. 5442 or by e-mail at
MacmillanSpecialMarkets@macmillan.com.

Library of Congress Cataloging-in-Publication Data

Names: Mills, Claudia, author.
Title: Write this down / Claudia Mills.
Description: New York : Farrar Straus Giroux, 2016. | Summary: "Twelve-
    year-old Autumn wants more than anything to be a real author, but
    when she wins a contest by writing something too personal about her
    brother, she has to decide if her dreams are more important than their
    relationship"—Provided by publisher.
Identifiers: LCCN 2015036615 | ISBN 978-1-250-14391-4 (paperback)
    ISBN 978-0-374-30166-8 (ebook)
Subjects: | CYAC: Authorship—Fiction. | Brothers and sisters—Fiction. |
    BISAC: JUVENILE FICTION / School & Education. | JUVENILE
    FICTION / Family / Siblings.
Classification: LCC PZ7.M63963 Wr 2016 | DDC [Fic]—dc23
LC record available at https://lccn.loc.gov/2015036615

Originally published in the United States by Farrar Straus Giroux
First Square Fish edition, 2018
Book designed by Roberta Pressel
Square Fish logo designed by Filomena Tuosto

3   5   7   9   10   8   6   4

AR: 5.7 / LEXILE: 890L

To my brilliant editor,
Margaret Ferguson,
with love

1

Here's the best thing about being a writer: it's like having a magic wand to make whatever you want happen to imaginary people in a made-up world.

Here's the worst thing about being a writer: it makes you wish even more that you had a magic wand to make whatever you want happen to actual people in your own real life.

I'm propped up in bed on a rainy October morning, sipping my special writing beverage, Swiss Miss hot chocolate, in the mug my brother, Hunter, gave me for my twelfth birthday this past April. The mug says, "Please do not annoy the writer. She may put you in a book and kill you."

It's hard to think of a mug much better than this one. Or a brother much better than one who would buy it for his writer sister.

And that's the kind of brother Hunter used to be: the best brother in the world. But everything's changed between us since school started back in August, tenth grade for Hunter, seventh grade for me. And I don't have a magic wand to make things be the way they were before.

I still love the mug, though, especially when it has hot chocolate in it, topped with a swirl of whipped cream squirted from one of those cans that don't look big enough to have that much whipped cream inside. I emptied one once out of curiosity when I was little, and believe me, there is a lot of whipped cream in there.

I'm writing a chapter in the first novel in my fantasy trilogy about this princess named Tatiana and her (very cute) wizard enemy, Ingvar. The problem is that I don't know what's going to happen next. I know Tatiana has to have more adventures, but she's already been in an earthquake, and her father, the king, was murdered by Ingvar's uncle, and she's just discovered an amulet—that's a magical object that protects her from harm. But if she has the amulet, nothing too bad can happen to her, and I'm only on chapter three, so maybe she has to lose the amulet somewhere, but it seems too soon for her to lose it when she's only had it for two and a half pages. But if she has it, how can she have adventures? And without adventures, I have no plot.

So I put aside the novel, which I'm scribbling on a yellow legal pad, and open my newest Moleskine notebook. I love Moleskine notebooks so much, with their creamy narrow-ruled paper and limp, soft covers tied shut with a slim black elastic ribbon. I fill a Moleskine notebook every month with poems, journal entries, story ideas, bits of dialogue, and descriptions that pop into my head that I don't want to forget.

On the first, beautifully blank page I write the opening line of a poem. Okay, not just a *poem*, but a new love poem for this boy, Cameron Miller, who sits next to me in journalism. A lot of kids think he's weird, but I have a huge crush on him. He's older than the rest of us because his parents took him out of school for a year to travel around the world—Paris! Buenos Aires! Beijing!—so he fell behind on a bunch of academic stuff. But he's way ahead of us in everything else.

I'm not going to show any of these poems to Cameron, of course. I'm not a completely clueless person who thinks the way you get a middle school boy to like you is to write poems for him. I'd never show my Cameron poems to anybody except my best friend, Kylee Willis, who is the only person I can share everything with, however mortifying. Kylee is the most calm and comforting person I've ever known. I bet she's awake, too, on this rainy morning, and thinking what a perfect day this is for knitting. Kylee is an amazing knitter. She can make scarves, hats, mittens, even sweaters.

Anyway, I keep my Cameron poems hidden away like Emily Dickinson did with hers. When I die, the poems can be published posthumously, which is a great word I learned that means "after my death." Everyone will say how tragic it is that I died so young. In these fantasies, I haven't totally worked out what I die from. In the books I like from long ago, it would be consumption, which nobody dies from anymore. The important part of the fantasy is how sad it will be that I died so young and that Cameron didn't even know of my love. He'll read the poems after they're published and finally know that the girl who sat next to him in journalism was the next Emily Dickinson. And then he'll wish he had said something to me other than "Hey" or "How's it going?"

But unless I die young, which I don't really want to happen, he's never going to read my poems, because I'd die if he did, unless I knew for a fact that he'd think they were wonderful and that he liked me, too. But if he thought they were pathetic—or if he thought I was pathetic for writing them—I would totally, completely, absolutely wither up and *expire*. So one way or another, if Cameron reads my poems it will either mean that I'm going to die any minute or that I'm already dead.

So Emily Dickinson is the role model for me.

I take another sip of hot chocolate, wiping the whipped cream from the tip of my nose with the back of my hand. And I keep on writing.

Three poems later, I go downstairs to toast myself an English muffin. While I was writing my Cameron poems I also had a mental breakthrough about the plot for my novel. Instead of trying to figure out how Tatiana can face exciting dangers if she has a magical amulet to protect her, I can take *out* the amulet scene and move it to *later* in the book. I know this sounds like the most obvious fix in the world now that I've said it, but when it comes to writing, things that seem obvious as soon as I think of them never seem obvious until after I think of them.

My parents are sitting at the kitchen table eating egg-white omelets crammed full of veggies. My father is an orthodontist, and now that I have braces, he's *my* orthodontist, too. His orthodontist name is Dr. Jaws, which he thinks is catchier than Dr. Granger. He must be right, because half of the kids at school who have braces go to my dad. His office also has a shark theme. If you want to make my dad go absolutely crazy with joy, buy him another grinning stuffed shark he can take to work, or come up with a new design for a shark-shaped Dr. Jaws refrigerator magnet.

My mother is a stay-at-home mom. She used to work as an administrator at the university, which she called "herding cats," as professors don't like being made to do anything they don't want to do. She quit her job a couple of years ago because she read in a pamphlet she picked up somewhere—"Surviving the Teen Years: A Guide for Parents"—that the teen years are actually the most important years to stay home with your kids, because that's when "things can happen." "Things can happen" might be code for "Your kids can start acting the way Hunter has been acting lately."

"Good morning!" Dad says.

This greeting could sound sarcastic if I said it to Hunter when he staggered out of bed past noon. Or it could just be an ordinary way of saying hello. But when Dad says it, he says it with gusto.

"Good morning!" I reply with equal gusto. It's not fake gusto, either, because I just wrote three poems and had a plot breakthrough. If that's not a good morning, I don't know what is.

Mom beams. She doesn't have as much gusto as Dad—

few people do—but she's happiest when the rest of us are happy, which is probably the definition of being a nice person. My mother is the second-nicest person I know. The first-nicest is Kylee.

"What plans do you have for today, Autumn?" she asks.

I shrug. Not a sullen Hunter shrug, but a mellow shrug of having a whole day to look forward to when there's nothing I *have* to do.

"I guess I won't be raking the leaves," Dad says, looking out at the rain. He doesn't sound disappointed.

"The band is practicing this afternoon," Mom says.

"Here?" Dad asks uneasily.

I know both my parents think the band might be part of the reason Hunter is different now. The other guys in the band are older than he is—juniors and seniors. But maybe he changed first and *then* joined the band. I'm not sure.

Even though my parents are suspicious of the band, they still let them practice in our house, down in the basement rec room. It's Mom's fault. She told Dad how important it is during the teen years that parents know where their kids are and what they're doing. The best way to do that is to make your home a welcoming place for your teenager and his friends. "If Hunter has to be in a rock band," I

9

heard her tell Dad, "better that they practice here, don't you think?"

Now Dad gives a sigh. "Hot stock tip," he says. "Invest in a company that sells earplugs."

He laughs, and Mom joins in, so I laugh, too. Because the band really does play very *very* loud.

The band members start to trickle in around three. The name of the band is Paradox, and it has four people in it. The lead guitar and lead vocalist just happens to be David Miller, which is to say—drum roll—Cameron's older brother. If Cameron were in a rock band, I bet he'd be its lead everything, too. Maybe he's too cool to be in a rock band, even though rock bands are definitely cool. But if he *were* in a band, he'd probably write the songs for it. He's one of the best writers in our journalism class.

The backup guitar and vocalist is Timber Jones, who has an Afro that I think he gets permed; it's albino white, with one purple streak in it, except sometimes the purple streak is green.

The bass player is Moonbeam Rollins. I'm sure he gave himself that first name. He reminds me of this poem we read in school, "Miniver Cheevy." In the poem, Miniver Cheevy, "born too late," wishes he lived in the Middle

Ages. Moonbeam wishes he lived in 1968. He wears tie-dyed T-shirts, sandals even in the winter, and a big peace sign on a chain around his neck.

Hunter is the drummer. He wanted to be a drummer back in fifth grade when kids got to choose what to play for instrumental music. But my dad said he had to do a "real instrument," so he was a trombone player for two years before he refused to be in the school band anymore. Then this past summer he found a drum set super cheap at a yard sale down the street, and the rest, as they say, is history.

The first couple of times the band came over, I holed up in my room or headed over to Kylee's. But lately I can't resist hanging around the band because of Cameron's brother being right here, in our house, in our kitchen, scarfing down the seven-layer dip Mom makes for them, with those tortilla chips that are little scoopers that break off into crumbly pieces and stick in your braces, speaking from unfortunate experience. I'm never in the kitchen with them—Hunter would hate that—but I sit in the family room just off the kitchen, pretending to be writing. Part of me hopes David will see me or at least cast his eyes in my direction as I'm musing over my manuscript.

Okay, this is pathetic, but today I even changed into a

flowy white dress, because Emily Dickinson always wore white dresses. My plan, or rather my dream, is that David's eyes will fall on me as I'm writing, all Emily-Dickinson-ish, and then maybe he'll say something about it to Cameron later.

"Hey, lil bro, is there a girl in your class named Summer or something?"

"Autumn. There's a girl in my journalism class named Autumn."

"That's right. Autumn. Well, she was writing all the time I was there, I mean, just totally lost in writing her story."

"Yeah, she's like that in journalism, too."

"I think the two of you have a lot in common. You both like to write, you're both sensitive, you're both mysterious . . ."

No. Even I can't imagine any world, however fantastic, in which this conversation actually happens. Besides, none of the band members, including David, can even see me from the kitchen, and they're deep in conversation about the band, talking about what they'd play at a gig if they ever got a gig. From what I overhear, it'd mainly be covers for songs by well-known bands, as well as songs by some indie groups, and maybe a couple of originals.

"Do you have a piece of paper I can use to write down

the playlist?" one of them asks. I think it's Timber. His voice is the deepest.

"There's got to be one around here somewhere," Hunter says.

"Can we just rip out a page from this notebook?" Moonbeam asks. "It looks like a fancy one, though."

OMG.

I left my Moleskine on the kitchen table after lunch.

The notebook with my Cameron poems that I wrote this morning.

Including the one titled "Ode to Cameron."

I should leap off the couch, race into the kitchen, and snatch the notebook from their hands before anyone can peek inside. But I'm paralyzed, like a squirrel spied by a dog who freezes into a squirrel-shaped statue.

"It's my sister's," Hunter says. I hear the sneer in his voice. This is not the voice of someone who bought me a perfect "Don't annoy the writer" mug only a few months ago.

Don't open it. Don't open it. Don't open it.

"Hey," Hunter says, and he's chuckling now, "get this."

No.

No.

No.

"'Ode to Cameron,'" he reads in a fake high voice.

All the air is sucked out of my lungs as if Hunter's words are a whooshing vacuum cleaner.

"'Ode to Cameron'?" David asks. "As in my brother Cameron?"

There isn't any other Cameron in our school.

Hunter keeps reading in the same warbly falsetto. "'If thou wouldst die, the snow would yield / yet another grave for me.'"

Laughter.

Are those such terrible lines? I'd like to see Hunter write anything a tenth as good. But they definitely sound terrible read aloud by Hunter with the other guys cracking up.

Hunter continues: "'If thou wouldst leave, my heart would break / like a ship wrecked on the sea.'"

Puking sounds. I cover my ears. Is Hunter the one pretending to puke? Or are the other guys fake-puking, too, including David?

Now my heart *is* broken, *exactly* like a ship wrecked on the sea.

I can never face Cameron again. Ever, ever, ever.

And I can never forgive Hunter. Ever, ever, ever.

If Hunter still liked me, even the tiniest, teensiest bit,

he could never make fun of me—of my writing!—in front of all his friends, including Cameron's brother.

I can't bear it anymore. I can't.

Even though the damage has already been done, I'm there in the kitchen now, grabbing at the notebook as Hunter, guffawing, holds it above my head, too high for me to reach.

"Give it back!" I shriek. "Give it *back*!"

From the corner of my eye, I can see Timber doubled over with laughter, but Moonbeam gives me a sheepish look.

"C'mon, Hunter, give it back to her," David says.

David!

With utter contempt, Hunter tosses my notebook onto the floor so that I have to crouch down to pick it up in the most humiliating way.

All four boys are silent now, watching me. But my eyes are fastened on Hunter, even though he's looking away, perhaps smarting from David's comment. He must know what a mean thing he just did.

"I'm going to publish my poems someday," I tell him. My voice starts out wobbly and quavery, but it gets louder and stronger as I keep on talking. "I'm going to be a famous writer, and *then* you'll be sorry you ever made fun of me.

I'm going to write something about *you*, and the whole world will read it and know what a terrible brother you turned into!"

Then I stumble out of the room. And I do mean stumble. My Emily Dickinson dress is too long, so I catch my heel on it and trip against the kitchen table, whacking my knee so hard my eyes sting with tears.

2

So let's brainstorm options," I tell Kylee as I'm lying on her bed clutching her very pink stuffed elephant to my very flat chest. I texted Kylee that I needed to come over and told my mom I was going to her house, but I didn't tell Mom what had happened. It's too humiliating to tell anyone in the world except for Kylee.

"Option number one," I say. "I transfer to another school. Immediately."

Kylee shakes her head so hard her dark bangs fall over her eyes. "You'd have to start all new classes, and you'd be behind already in everything, and your best friend would miss you every minute of the day, and your parents would never let you."

"Right now we're brainstorming," I remind her. "Brainstorming means you think of everything, every single option, good and bad, without passing judgment on any of them. Like we did in Mr. Harris's language arts class last year."

Besides, option number one sounds pretty good to me, at least compared to the option of going into journalism on Monday and facing Cameron after his brother heard my love poem. Even though David was the nicest to me of any of them, I can't imagine that he won't tell Cameron about it.

"So what's option number two?" Kylee's eyes stay fastened on me, her fingers effortlessly clicking her knitting needles down the next row of the pink-and-green-and-yellow scarf she's knitting. She's such a good knitter she doesn't have to pay attention while she knits.

"Option number two is I drop journalism." I'd still have to see Cameron in the halls, but that's totally different from sitting right next to him in class every single day.

"No!" Kylee moans. "That's your favorite subject! And then we'd only have two classes together!"

She obviously didn't listen to my reminder about brainstorming.

"Option number three," I continue, but I can't think of a third way to avoid having to see Cameron ever again for the rest of my life. "Run away?"

"That isn't funny." Now Kylee's distressed enough that she puts down her knitting. "Option number *three* is that you forget about it. I'd bet you anything that David won't even tell Cameron. Girls talk about boys a lot more than boys talk about girls."

Kylee herself never talks about boys. She doesn't have a crush on anyone, though there's this very short, mega-awkward boy named Henry Dubin who has a crush on her; he's in science with Kylee, and art. You can tell he likes her because he always seems to be bumping her with his backpack in the hall and snorting in this high-pitched horsey kind of way.

Now I have to hope that Cameron's brother doesn't joke with him about me the way I joke with Kylee about Henry Dubin.

I can so see the scene playing itself out in my mind. Cameron's brother sits down to dinner with Cameron and their parents in the ultra-modern-looking house where they live, a few blocks from us, the house I walk by every chance I get, always pretending I'm on the way to somewhere else.

"Hey, lil bro, is there a girl in your class named Summer or something?"

"Autumn. There's a girl in my journalism class named Autumn."

"That's right. Autumn. Well, she has a big-time crush on you, man."

"You're kidding."

"Nope. I was at her brother's house today with the band. And her brother, Hunter, read us one of her poems. And guess what it was called? 'Ode to Cameron.'"

Gagging noises from Cameron.

"She's really nuts about you. Listen to this. Are you ready?"

Sickening silence from Cameron, who is not at all ready.

"'If thou wouldst croak, the snow would puke up yet another grave for me.' Or something like that."

Awkward laughter from Cameron. "Man. Oh, man. It's bad enough that she's always staring at me in journalism class. Oh, man, this sucks."

This scene is a lot more believable than my dumb Emily Dickinson fantasy. Its dialogue sounds completely real, while the other one sounded fake.

But maybe, maybe David will tell Cameron the *real* opening lines from my poem and Cameron will think they're *good*? Maybe he's secretly liked me all along and will be glad to know I secretly like him?

Kylee has gone back to her knitting, but I know she's still thinking.

"Okay," she says when she gets to the end of another row. "Option number four—well, maybe this is just the same as *my* option number three—is that you act normal around him tomorrow, and the next day, and the next day, and the day after that. I really don't think Cameron's brother is going to talk to Cameron about you, and if he does, he can't say your poems are bad, because they aren't bad—they're wonderful."

Did I mention that I love Kylee more than anyone in the world? I do have other friends. Sometimes I go over to Isabelle Abshire's house to watch old black-and-white movies, because Kylee won't watch anything that isn't in color. Sometimes Brianna Clark hangs out with Kylee and me; she once said we're "soothing" to be around, but I know she really meant Kylee. But I love Kylee a thousand times more than I love either of them.

So Kylee just said my poems are wonderful. Despite the horribleness of everything that happened, down deep— well, not even down all that deep—I still think they're wonderful, too.

"What if . . ." I begin, and then trail off. "Kylee, tell me honestly. I know best friends are supposed to believe in each other, but they're supposed to be honest with each other, too. Do you really, truly, cross-your-heart-and-hope-to-die think my poems are good—and not just my poems generally, but my Cameron poems?"

Without a moment of hesitation, Kylee nods.

"What if—maybe this is ridiculous . . ." I say, even though I don't think it's ridiculous because it's what I've been planning to do ever since I made my big announcement to Hunter and the band this afternoon, just sooner than I thought.

"In brainstorming, nothing is ridiculous," Kylee reminds me.

"What if I published my poems somewhere? Somewhere really impressive? And then it won't matter what Hunter said, or what Cameron *might* say, because a famous poetry magazine will be on record saying that they're fabulous. And Hunter will be like, *Wow, I guess Autumn really can write, and I shouldn't have made fun of her.* And Cameron will be like, *Wow, I guess this majorly published poet is a girl I'd like to get to know.*"

Just this morning I wanted to be like Emily Dickinson and not publish my poems until after I die. A lot can change in a few hideous hours.

"Now you're talking!" Kylee said, though maybe she's just so relieved that I'm not going to change schools or drop journalism or run away that she's acting more enthusiastic than she really feels. But Kylee is a terrible liar, so I know she means whatever she says.

I let myself play out a new script in my head.

"Hey, lil bro, is there a girl in your class named Summer or something?"

"Autumn. There's a girl in my journalism class named Autumn."

"That's right. Autumn. Well, she has a big-time crush on you, man."

Silence from Cameron, who is blushing with secret pleasure.

"She wrote a poem about you."

"She did?"

"Her brother made fun of it, but I thought it was really good. I bet she'll be a famous published poet someday."

Cameron gives a slow smile. "I think so, too."

3

When I get home, the band has finally left—hooray, hooray. I google "most prestigious places to publish poetry" on the computer in my room. A long list comes up, showing that I am hardly the first person in the history of the world to ask this question. In fact, one site lists fifty places. Fifty! Number one on the list, and the only one I've heard of, is this magazine called *The New Yorker,* which my parents get even though we live in Colorado and not in New York. It comes to our house every week, and my mother reads it. I don't know if she reads the poems; the magazine publishes stories, articles, and cartoons, too, all kinds of stuff. When she's done with it, Dad takes the old copies to his office waiting room so parents have something to read while their kids are getting their braces tightened.

The Internet list of prestigious poetry places says that

The New Yorker has a million readers. A million! So that's what I'm going to start with, on the theory that you might as well aim high. I read this saying once, "If you aim at the stars, at least you won't shoot your foot off."

I'm not exactly sure how that applies here, but I do know that it would be lovely to walk into journalism with *The New Yorker* tucked under my arm. I'd shyly show it to Ms. Archer, who would say, *Class! Class! I have some wonderful news to share! Autumn—yes,* our *Autumn—has a poem published in* The New Yorker! I'd still feel a teensy bit embarrassed when she'd start to read "Ode to Cameron"— maybe I should change his name before I send it in?—but a person who gets her poems published in the most prestigious place there is doesn't have much reason to be embarrassed about anything ever again.

I go back downstairs, completely ignoring Hunter, who is zoned out in front of a *Simpsons* rerun on TV, and retrieve the latest *New Yorker* from my mother's always overflowing pile of books and magazines. Back in my room, I flip through the issue to see what the poems are like.

I have to admit I don't understand any of them.

Even worse: not a single one rhymes.

What do modern poets have against rhyme? Rhyme is wonderful! It gives a poem structure. It delights the ear.

Robert Frost, who wrote that famous poem about stopping by woods on a snowy evening, said writing poems without rhyme is like playing tennis without a net.

Maybe there's a connection between the fact that poets nowadays write poems that don't rhyme and that poets nowadays write poems nobody wants to read. People in my classes at school moan and groan whenever we begin a poetry unit. I think they're afraid they won't understand the poems and somebody—say, a teacher—will put them on the spot in front of everybody and ask them to explain what the poem means.

But my Cameron poems aren't like that. What they mean is perfectly clear. They mean I love Cameron.

If I send my Cameron poems to *The New Yorker*, will they reject them because my poems rhyme and are easy to understand? Or will the editors say: *Someone* finally *sent us poems that rhyme! And, look, we can even figure out what they mean!*

I won't know unless I try.

On the computer I search for "*New Yorker*" and "submissions." It turns out that sending my poems off to *The New Yorker* will be as easy as pie. You can submit poems online, up to six poems at one time. Does this mean they'd publish all six, or just pick the one they like best? Well, either way, it just so happens I have six Cameron poems written already.

I continue reading and find some more disturbing information: the website says that they review submissions "on a rolling basis" (which is good, since it means you can submit poems anytime) but that it can take "two to six months" to get a response.

Two to six months! It's October 1 now. Am I supposed to have to wait all the way until December or even March?

Well, if I have to wait that long to show Hunter that at least one of my poems has been published in the fanciest magazine in America, then that's what I have to do. If I have to wait that long to trot into journalism class with my glorious published poem to share with Cameron, I'd better type up my six poems and send them off to *The New Yorker* today.

And I do.

I don't change Cameron's name either. If I become a famous love poet, I might as well be famous for writing "the Cameron poems," not "poems for some boy with a made-up name."

Plus, I love Cameron's name, and not just because I love everything about him. He has a poetic name, unlike poor Henry Dubin. I can't imagine publishing "the Henry Dubin poems."

But "the Cameron poems"—that's an entirely different story.

I close my eyes and see one of them printed right there in *The New Yorker* already.

4

It's Monday, and I'm heading to my second-period class: journalism. I feel tingly nervousness every day when I walk into class knowing I'm going to see Cameron, but I feel it even more today at the thought that he might have heard my poem and made fun of it. Or heard my poem and thought it was wonderful. Or maybe he didn't think anything about my poem at all.

He's already there, hunched over his journalism notebook. He's doodling, and his doodles are super intricate and detailed. I think they should be hung in an art museum. He wears his hair longer than most of the other boys, not too long, but reaching past the collar of the Oxford-weave button-down shirts he wears every day (not grungy T-shirts), and his bangs cover his left eye.

Ms. Archer had us sit in the same seats every day at the

start of the school year to help her learn our names, and now we sit in the same seats every day from habit. There's really no way I could switch seats now—it would be too bizarre—so I make myself sit down at the desk next to Cameron, who is right by the window. Kylee's on my other side, but she's not here yet because she has P.E. first period, which is really gross, because then you're sweaty for the rest of the day. There are showers in the locker room but nobody—*nobody*—has ever—*ever*—used them. I'm lucky I have P.E. seventh period, so only the kids in my eighth-period science class have to smell me.

So right now it's me and Cameron.

Right now it's Cameron and me.

I usually don't speak to him first; I wait to see if he's going to speak to me.

Sometimes he does, but he just says hi, and sometimes he doesn't even *say* it, just gives me a sort of salute with his left hand (he's left-handed) or a brief nod.

Today he doesn't. Not a good sign.

I make a big show of opening my journalism binder and pretending to look at my notes from last week on Q&A interview pieces. Yet I can't help but take a peek at what he's doodling. It's a complicated pattern of autumn leaves. I know they're autumn leaves because he doodles with colored pencils—he has a set of twenty-four pencils, all perfectly sharpened—and he's using two shades of red and two shades of orange.

Autumn leaves. Like me, Autumn?

Maybe this is a good sign. Maybe it means David told him about my poem, and he knows I like him, and he's starting to wonder if he also likes me.

Kylee arrives, panting into her seat just as the bell rings. She looks at me, her eyes big with questions. But I don't have any answers, so I shrug, and class begins.

Ms. Archer gives us a warm, welcoming smile. She is my favorite teacher ever. She's beautiful, with flawless, warm brown skin, short-cropped hair, huge dark eyes, and impossibly long earrings she wears to go with her flowing skirts. I'd love to dress exactly like her, but my mom won't let me wear big earrings, and if I wore skirts like hers it would be pathetically obvious I was trying to copy her. But someday, when I won't *look* so much like a copycat, I'm going to *be* a total copycat, and dress that way.

But she's my favorite teacher not because of how she looks. She knows everything there is to know about writing. She's published poems in literary magazines, and she wrote a short story that was picked for a collection of best stories from the West. And she's not just smart, she's

31

wise, even though she's not super old—maybe in her late twenties.

For a moment I wish I could tell her about Hunter and Cameron and everything, to see what she'd say. But I don't want her to think I'm weird and my family even weirder.

"Good morning, class," Ms. Archer says, once she has our attention. "Today we're going to start our two-week unit on personal essays, short pieces that tell the reader a true personal experience of the writer. I'm going to start us off by saying something that may strike you as surprising. Are you ready for this? Even though you'll be sharing personal experiences, a personal essay is not about *you*."

I write that down in my binder. I'm a good note taker anyway, but especially in Ms. Archer's class I try to write down every word she says. Cameron doesn't take notes; he spends most of class gazing out the window or doodling, even though I know from how good a writer he is that he must listen to Ms. Archer, unless he knows everything she says already. Kylee doesn't take notes either. She asked Ms. Archer if it was okay if she knits in class, and Ms. Archer said yes. Kylee listens best when she's knitting.

"Do people want to read a personal essay to learn about *you*?" Ms. Archer asks. Right away she answers her own question. "No. Unless you're already famous, they have no idea who you are. They don't have any reason yet to care about you or anything you've experienced."

Tyler Shields, who sits in front of me, calls out, "Then why do they read it?" Tyler is the best in the class at direct, blunt questions the rest of us would be too embarrassed to ask.

Ms. Archer turns to the class. "Anybody? Personal essays are loved by many readers. I know I turn first to a personal essay whenever I pick up a magazine or a newspaper. Why?"

The room is silent, except for the soft, steady, rhythmic click of Kylee's needles.

No one volunteers to answer until Olivia Fernandez lifts her hand into the air. Olivia is a terrific writer, but there's something about her that sets my teeth on edge. Maybe it's just that she *is* a terrific writer and I'm jealous? Okay, I'm jealous. But she's also just so sure of herself all the time; she's always the one waving a hand in the air— except she doesn't *wave* it; she raises it in this slow, almost leisurely way. Oh, and in addition to being a fabulous writer, she's also gorgeous. Like, model-level gorgeous, with waist-length raven-black hair, a glowing olive complexion, and impossibly blue eyes. I don't think she likes Cameron the way I do, but if she did, my chances with him would be pretty much nil.

"Personal essays have a *theme*," Olivia says. "They take the writer's personal experience and find some *universal truth* in it."

"Good, Olivia. Very good," Ms. Archer says.

I think I might have something to add, but I've become shy in this class because I don't want to say something dumb in front of Ms. Archer or Cameron. But Ms. Archer is good at reading faces, and mine must be giving me away, because she says, "Autumn?"

I swallow hard before I make myself answer. "People like to read personal essays because they don't feel so alone then? Someone else has made it through the same thing they're going through. Or maybe it's a different thing, but it's still hard. Or maybe . . ." I'm not sure if what I'm saying makes any sense. I wonder if Cameron is looking over at me as I'm speaking; my hands feel sweaty, as if I just came from P.E. like Kylee. "It's just so *real*—someone else felt something so *real*. Maybe it's *not* a bad thing, or a hard thing, but it's a *real* thing, and the reader is feeling real things, too, and so he or she doesn't feel alone."

Now I can't help but glance over at Cameron to see if he's nodding, but he's still hunched over his doodles. Maybe he wasn't even listening to anything I said. Kylee is nodding, of course. Olivia whispers something I can't hear to Kaitlyn Ellis, who sits next to her—something snarky? She can be snarky sometimes.

A moment goes by as Ms. Archer lets my comments settle. Then she smiles again.

"Exactly. People read personal essays to learn something about *themselves*."

She goes on to tell us that personal essays are about *two* things: the thing that happened, and what it *means*. If you just write about something that happens, without having it mean anything, what you have is an "incident," and that's not enough for a personal essay. But you can't explain the meaning in any super-obvious way, like stories for little kids that spell out the moral at the end. You have to be subtle. You have to say it without saying it.

"Okay," she says. "Now that I've totally overwhelmed you, let's do a freewrite."

She has us do freewrites in class a couple of times a week. She doesn't read them or grade them; they're just for us, to turn on our writing brains and get our writing juices flowing.

"Forget everything I just said," Ms. Archer goes on. "Don't worry yet about what anything means. That will come later. It's better if it comes later. I'm going to give you a prompt, and I want you to do nothing for the next ten minutes but see where that prompt leads you."

She picks up the chalk and writes on the board: "The worst—or best—gift you ever received."

I make a brainstorming list, starting with the worst gifts because bad things are always good to write about. I think best when I have a pen in my hand. Sometimes it feels like I have to have a pen in my hand in order even to *think*, that I don't even *have* an idea until I write it down.

Mitten, I write. That was the name of the guinea pig I got for Christmas when I was nine; he died a week later.

Electric toothbrush. From my dad, of course.

Holes, *the book.* It's a great book, but Aunt Liz sent it to me three years in a row. She must really like it.

Okay, now I should try to think of some good gifts.

My first Moleskine notebook. That was my best-ever gift, from Kylee, two birthdays ago.

My writer mug from Hunter.

Kylee is still knitting, but I can tell from the way her forehead is scrunched up that she's ready to leap into writing soon.

Olivia turns around and shoots her an annoyed look, as if the click of Kylee's needles is keeping her from coming up with an amazing bad gift/good gift idea. This time I hear what she whispers, while jerking her thumb in Kylee's direction: "Granny." She and Kaitlyn both crack up, but they snicker so quietly that Ms. Archer doesn't notice.

I feel my face flushing with sudden heat. I don't think Kylee heard, and if she did, she probably wouldn't care. She'd just say, *My grandma loved to knit, and I'm glad I'm like her.* If she knew how angry I feel right now at Olivia, she'd be puzzled, like, *Who cares what Olivia thinks about anything?* That is another huge difference between Kylee and me. And maybe I wouldn't care if Olivia said something like that about *me*—except that I would—but I totally care if she says it about *Kylee.* I think when we love someone we care about them more than we do about ourselves.

Suddenly, I know what I want to write about.

I want to write about my best gift *ever.*

Now I can't stop my pen from flying across the page.

I'm five, and I'm afraid of the dark, because as soon as it's dark, there's this cubbyhole in my bedroom under the eaves behind a little square door with a little round doorknob, and when it's totally dark, the doorknob turns, and the door creaks open, and

Mrs. Whistlepuff comes out. She's all made of a cold, cold wind, a bad-smelling wind, like the wind that blows in from a garbage dump. She tries to blow my covers off, and no matter how I pull on them to hold them tight, I can feel her tugging, too. I know if she gets the covers off, she'll breathe on me, and if Mrs. Whistlepuff breathes on you, you die. I can't scream because Mrs. Whistlepuff sucks all my breath away, and I can't tell my parents because my father took the night-light out of my room because five-year-olds are big girls who don't need night-lights anymore. I have to be a big girl now, even if it means Mrs. Whistlepuff is going to kill me.

The only person I tell is Hunter. He's eight, and he's not afraid of anything.

He doesn't laugh. He doesn't say, "There's no such person as Mrs. Whistlepuff."

He rides his bike all by himself to the store a few blocks from our house and comes back with something hidden under his jacket. My parents don't know where he went, and they're furious, and they take his bike away for a week, because he's not allowed to leave without letting them know where he's going.

The thing he had hidden under his coat is a flash-
light. For me. And batteries, too, and he even knew
which kind of batteries to get, and how to put the bat-
teries in, with the plus and minus ends in the right
place, and everything.

Now when it's dark, dark, dark in my room, and
I hear the doorknob turn and the door start to creak
open, I shine the flashlight over to the cubby, and Mrs.
Whistlepuff has to go back inside and stay there.

And she never bothers me again.

The end.

Except it's not the end. The end is how Hunter read my poem aloud to his friends, and they all laughed.

I don't have that flashlight anymore. I'm not sure if Hunter bought it for me with his birthday money or swiped it the way he swiped a chocolate bar—and got in big trouble—a few weeks later.

I just remember how bright its beam was.

I just remember how it let me be safe in my bed again through the night.

Cameron is writing now, too, intently bent over his page, his hand at that awkward angle left-handed people use when they write. I still don't know what he's writing about. He acted pretty normal today, all things considered—that is to say, normal for someone who isn't like anybody else I've ever known. Maybe David took pity on me and didn't tell him? Maybe David told him, and Cameron didn't even care?

Somehow that last possibility seems the worst of all.

5

After school on Tuesday I'm sitting in the backseat of my mom's Subaru Outback, eyes scrunched shut, waiting to die.

"Hunter," Mom says to my brother, who is at the wheel. "You need to check the mirrors. *All* the mirrors. Rearview mirror. *Both* side mirrors."

"There's nothing to see!" he snaps. "We haven't even left the driveway yet!"

"And we're not *going* to leave the driveway until you do as I say."

Our mother isn't generally the control-freak type. It's more that she's overprotective. When Hunter and I were little kids getting ready to cross the street, she'd make us look both ways not once but twice. Look left, look right, look left again, look right again, and *then* we could put one toe off the sidewalk.

"Why don't you drive, Mom?" I suggest, opening my eyes. Usually I keep completely quiet in the car when Hunter is driving, both because I think he needs all his concentration to avoid killing us, and also because I feel embarrassed for him, having to learn such a big, new hard thing with an audience watching every single minute. But I'm still furious about his meanness to me last weekend. My Mrs. Whistlepuff freewrite only made me even angrier at this new, nasty Hunter who showed up at the start of the school year and took my real, true brother away.

"Why don't you shut up, Autumn?" Hunter says.

He didn't use to say things like that to me. He used to say things like that to other kids when they picked on me for being too tall, too skinny, too quick to cry. Years ago, when Charlie Munch on our street called me "Skinny Minnie," Hunter, without missing a beat, called him "Chunky Monkey," and just like that Charlie's nickname became "Chunk" *forever.*

"Hunter, don't talk that way to your sister," Mom says. To me she says, "He has to log fifty hours behind the wheel before he can get his license. There's no way he can get that many hours if he doesn't do some of the driving when we go out on errands. Honey, check the mirrors so we can go."

Hunter gives a huge sigh, but he does look in the general direction of the mirrors.

"Okay," Mom says. "Start backing out the driveway. Slowly."

The car leaps backward, like a racehorse galloping in reverse out of the gate.

Mom and I shriek simultaneously. "Brake!" she shouts. "Hunter, brake!"

Whiplash time. My head jerks forward as the car screeches to a halt, still in the driveway.

"*Ease* on the gas," she says. "Don't press the pedal down all the way. Just press it down a little bit."

"If I drive any slower, Autumn's going to be late to her orthodontist appointment," Hunter points out.

The appointment is at four, and it's already three forty-five, although we climbed into the car ten minutes ago. It took that long for Mom to give all the instructions that Hunter is ignoring. But the office is just ten minutes away, and it doesn't matter much if we're late when my ortho-dontist is also my dad. And it's not like Hunter cares whether I get there on time; he just wants Mom to stop talking and let him start driving.

"Better late than dead," I chirp.

Okay, I didn't need to say that. But he didn't need to tell me to shut up either.

"If thou wouldst shut thy trap," Hunter snaps, " 'twould be a most excellent idea."

Now, *that* was low. I cannot believe he's sitting there teasing me even more about my "Ode to Cameron."

I hate you, Hunter, I want to say, but Mom doesn't let us use words like "hate" or "stupid" or "shut up." Apparently "shut thy trap" is acceptable, or maybe she's too stressed with the driving lesson to notice.

So angry I can hardly breathe, I pull out my Moleskine notebook, which I'm never going to let out of my sight ever again. If I can't say what I want out loud, at least I can say it in writing.

Tuesday, October 4. Hunter driving, I write at the top of the page.

I cross out *Hunter driving* and write *Hunter trying to drive.*

The car is finally inching backward at a pace slow enough to satisfy Mom. But now we're at the end of the driveway, and Hunter is going to have to pull out into the street. Hunter can barely drive, let alone drive backward, not to mention turning backward into traffic. Okay, there isn't any traffic on our quiet cul-de-sac, but there *might* be.

I try to think of the best words to describe exactly how my insides feel, both from how Hunter is driving and from what he just said.

Butterflies fluttering. I cross it out. Cliché. Plus, butterflies are too sweet and gentle for this utter upheaval of emotion. More like *Elephants stampeding.*

Heart banging around in my chest like a tennis ball in a dryer. Great line. But as often happens when an especially wonderful line springs into my head, I have a bad feeling I read it in a book somewhere.

Hunter makes it out of the driveway, and we're on the street now, waiting at the stop sign to turn onto a bigger road, a road that will have actual cars on it driven by actual other drivers.

"No!" Mom's voice cuts through my thoughts as Hunter creeps forward. "Wait! Don't you see that Honda?"

"It's a million miles away! Maybe two million!"

"No, it's not!"

"Mom, I could have pulled out ten times already. Look, it's *still* a million miles away."

"Wait until I tell you. I mean it, Hunter. Wait!"

Heart beating against my ribs like a bird trapped in a too-small cage.

Stomach choked with molten lava about to erupt.

"Okay, *now*," Mom says.

The car gives another wild leap as Hunter makes his turn and starts to speed down the busier street.

"Slow down! Slow down! Slow down!"

Why has the road suddenly become incredibly narrow, the parked cars looming on the right, ongoing traffic hurtling toward us on the left?

"You're too close!" Mom reaches over and grabs the wheel. The car swings away from the parked brand-new Audi it was about to total and veers in the other direction over the centerline. I close my eyes and brace myself for the sound of the crash. But I squint one eye to see the two of them, four hands on the wheel, swing it back into our lane.

"Mom," Hunter says, "it's better to hit a parked car than a moving car."

"At least the moving car has a chance of getting out of the way," she fires back.

"Um, it's better not to hit either one," I say.

Hunter's ears flare red. I hope being mad won't hinder his efforts to avoid hitting anything.

Without taking his eyes off the road, he says, "You know what, Autumn, great critic of other people's driving? Thy poetry sucks. And guess who else thinks it sucks? Cameron's brother told me Cameron thought your poem sucked, too."

"Hunter," Mom says in a warning tone. "Suck" is another word on Mom's forbidden list.

But it's not the word I care about. Is Hunter telling me the truth? Did David really tell Cameron about my poem and Cameron thought it was bad?

I don't mind if the car crashes now, which it very well might.

"Hunter, it's a yellow light. Stop! It's going to change any second. Stop!"

Hunter accelerates and makes it through the light just before it turns red.

"See?" he crows as he zips close to an enormous truck barreling toward us from the opposite direction.

If only the *New Yorker* poetry editor read my poems the very first thing when he got to his office Monday morning and showed them to a bunch of other *New Yorker* poetry people, and they already decided to accept one for publication! If only he's emailing me right now to tell me! I know that can't happen—well, it *could* happen, but it would be ridiculously fast after they said "two to six months" on their website. But I glance at the email alert on my phone just in case.

Nothing.

Two minutes later I check again.

Still nothing.

6

It's dinnertime, with the whole family sitting at the table: me, Dad, Mom, and Hunter. We don't have dinner together every night in my family, because a lot of the time this year Hunter is hanging out with the band, and I have ballet or a flute lesson, or I'm at Kylee's house. But it means a lot to Mom that we try to sit down for dinner a few times a week.

My mother is taking a cooking class called Secrets of a Healthy Asian Kitchen, so she's made some kind of stir-fry with hormone-free chicken, lots of organic veggies, and brown rice, which is healthier than white rice. She's always reading up on nutrition and deciding that everything in our lives would go better if we were gluten free, or had less dairy, or ate more nuts and olive oil. The stir-fry smells yummy, but I never feel like eating anything after I've gotten my braces tightened.

"So who had a good day?" Mom asks.

Tonight I can't think of anything non-snarky to say.

I'm still alive despite having to drive with Hunter.

But I wish I weren't because Hunter might have ruined everything with Cameron forever with his totally hideous meanness.

So Mom answers her own question. "Hunter logged another half hour behind the wheel," she tells Dad. She didn't have a chance to talk to him at his office because parents wait in the waiting room, even parents who happen to be married to the orthodontist.

"Great!" Dad says. He gives Hunter a big thumbs-up.

"Derrick," Mom asks Dad then, "do you want to tell them, or should I?"

I can tell Dad has some extra-nice news of his own to share. He gives her a smiling go-ahead nod.

"The *Broomville Banner* readers' poll picked him as Broomville's Best Orthodontist again. This makes seven years in a row!"

Dad grins with pleasure. He works so hard at making braces fun for kids who might otherwise hate them that he totally deserves this.

"Yay!" I say, giving him a happy high five. Hunter has a mouthful of food and so can't offer any congratulations, but he manages a couple of feeble claps.

"Autumn?" Mom prompts, so I have to come up with something.

"I'm going to have a flute solo in the band concert next week," I finally say. Hunter gets meanest of all when I say anything even mildly braggy, even when it's just a fact I'm reporting about something nice that happened to me.

I was super happy about the flute solo until the car ride with Hunter and his bombshell about Cameron hating my poems. Now I can't be happy about anything.

"Great!" Dad says again. "How are your other classes going?"

Although the question is addressed to me, his eyes dart over to Hunter. But our parents already know how we're doing in our classes because our school district has this totalitarian thing called Infinite Campus, where parents can go online and check their kids' grades 24/7. Even though my grades are mostly A's, except for B's in math, it makes me feel strange to think of Mom and Dad monitoring them every second. And Hunter must absolutely hate it. He was never what you'd call a great student—his grades have always been mainly B's and C's—but since his big changeroo this year, they're slipping toward low C's, bordering on D's, because of all the work he doesn't even bother to finish and turn in.

"They're good," I say. If I mention I got the only A in the class on the last French test, Hunter will totally loathe and despise me. Still, I kind of want them to know. From Infinite Campus they'd know I got an A on the test; they wouldn't know I got the *only* A.

Maybe Hunter already hates me so much he can't really hate me any more.

"On the last French test? I got the only A in the class."

"Whoop-de-doo," Hunter says, as nasty as I knew he'd be.

"Hunter," Mom warns. Now she has a new word to add to the forbidden list: "Whoop-de-doo." Or maybe it's not the word that's a problem, but the *tone*, dripping with sarcasm.

Dad beams at me as if he hadn't heard Hunter's whoop-de-doo crack.

"Très bien," he says, pronouncing it wrong on purpose to be funny, saying "trehz bean" instead of "tray bee-en."

"How about you, Hunter?" he asks then. "Classes okay? Is Mrs. Pigusch starting to make Algebra Two any clearer?"

Hunter flushes. A month ago our parents hired a math tutor who comes to our house twice a week, a retired teacher who is hard of hearing and talks in a very loud voice the whole time, so that, upstairs in my room, I can hear practically every word. Hunter is in a fouler mood than ever on Mrs. Pigusch days.

Hunter doesn't answer.

"Well, we're barely into October," Mom says in her best soothing voice, as if Hunter were the one who had just expressed concern about his grades. "You still have plenty of time to bring things up before the end of the trimester."

"You know," Dad says, "when I was in middle school, I was close to failing math. But I decided that it wasn't my math *aptitude* that was the problem; it was my math *attitude*. Let me tell you, it made a world of difference. By the time I got to high school, I was sailing along. I even joined the math team."

"And now you're Broomville's best orthodontist seven years in a row." Hunter sneers, as if being an orthodontist is some kind of joke. "Wow, Dad. Talk about coming a long way."

The muscles tense in Dad's jaw, and Mom lays her hand on his arm, as if to warn him not to say what he might say next. Not that Dad ever says anything terrible to either one of us, but sometimes I can look at him, look at both of our parents, and know what they're thinking. And *thinking* can be even worse than *saying*.

My brother must know this, too, because he lays down his fork and stalks out of the room, leaving most of his healthy-Asian-kitchen meal uneaten on his plate.

7

I'm the one who sees the sign on the display board in front of the Broomville Humane Society. We're in the car: Mom is driving Kylee and me to our Thursday-afternoon ballet class.

I'm not very good at ballet, but Dad says I have to do a sport, and I got him to agree that ballet is athletic enough to count. Even though Dad tried to make Hunter do a sport, too, Hunter didn't do *any* extracurricular activities his freshman year, as in none at all. Dad made this big speech last summer about how what you do *after* school is just as important for getting into a good college as how you do *during* school, so this year Hunter signed up for cross-country, which doesn't require competitive tryouts like football (Dad's favorite sport) or soccer or tennis. But Hunter quit after the first week of practice, which started in August the week before school began; in fairness to Hunter, it *was* the hottest August ever recorded in Broom-ville. Dad, who usually rolls with life's punches pretty well, stalked out of the room when Hunter broke the news to him, just like Hunter stalked out of the room on the healthy-Asian-dinner night.

Kylee isn't very good at ballet either, and her parents don't care about sports, but they said she has to do some-thing besides knit all the time.

So twice a week, on Mondays and Thursdays, Kylee and I go together to this funky, run-down dance studio on the other side of town from the Dr. Jaws office. We have to pass the Humane Society building on the way there, and they have this sign in front that says things like ADOPTION SPECIAL THIS WEEK! or (on the week Hunter quit the cross-country team) DON'T LEAVE PETS IN A HOT CAR!

"Mom, stop!" I call from the backseat, where Kylee is sitting next to me.

Mom slams on the brakes, which is *not* what I meant for her to do, especially with a huge SUV right behind us.

I guess I should have made myself more clear.

Thankfully, she manages to pull over to the side of the road. Wouldn't it have been ironic if I survived Hunter's driving only to get myself killed in a rear-end collision with my safety-obsessed mother at the wheel?

"Autumn, don't shout things like that while I'm driving!" Mom scolds.

"I'm sorry," I say in a small voice because I really truly am. "I wanted Kylee to see the sign on the animal shelter."

Kylee reads it aloud: "KNIT FOR DOGS! DETAILS INSIDE!"

I expect Kylee's face to light up with excitement. The only thing Kylee loves as much as knitting is animals. Her parents won't let her get a pet—her mom's allergic—so this could be next best.

But she wrinkles her little button nose. I like Kylee's nose so much better than mine. Hers is cute. Mine is more what you'd call regal, which really means big and pointy-ish.

"Remember that penguin-knitting thing you found for me?" she asks. "Where I was supposed to knit sweaters for penguins who were injured in that oil spill in Australia or somewhere? You showed me pictures of penguins dressed up in sweaters, and so I knitted three whole penguin sweaters, and then we found out that penguins hate wearing sweaters, and being made to wear a sweater stresses already stressed-out, oil-soaked penguins even more?"

Okay, so knitting penguin sweaters had been a bad idea.

Even if the picture of the penguins in their sweaters had been quite possibly the most adorable picture in the history of the world.

"We should go in and get the details at least," I say. "Mom, can we? You know we're always super early for ballet."

"Kylee?" Mom asks.

Kylee shrugs. "Okay." But she crinkles her forehead in a skeptical way.

The lady at the front desk is knitting when we walk in. A good sign!

Margo—that's what it says on her name badge— explains that the warmth and snugness of a sweater is comforting for dogs who have been abandoned to an animal shelter. She says the shelter believes in taking their dogs out on exercise walks in all kinds of weather, and sweaters will be needed with cold weather on the way. She says the dogs can take their sweaters with them to their new homes when they're adopted, and the familiarity of the sweater helps ease the transition.

It makes perfect sense to me.

"Are all of you knitters?" Margo asks.

"Just Kylee," I say. "But Kylee is a totally amazing knitter."

"So what do you think, Kylee?" Margo asks. "We have a variety of patterns I can give you, sized for small, medium, and large dogs. And we have yarn donated by local merchants."

At that very moment, a shelter volunteer comes through the front door with three small dogs on leashes. The dogs are wearing hand-knit sweaters.

Kylee gives a big, deep, rapturous sigh. I sigh with relief at hearing her sigh.

Three minutes later she is clutching a folder of photocopied dog sweater patterns in one hand and a shopping bag filled with skeins of brightly colored yarn in the other.

"Girls, we're going to be late for ballet," Mom says, but she, too, seems dazzled by the adorableness of the dogs in their sweaters. Knowing my mother, now she'll try to teach herself to knit from some YouTube video—maybe we'd be a happy family if we all had matching hand-knit sweaters—only to give up on it a couple of weeks later. During which time, my best friend will have knitted sweaters for every dog in the Broomville animal shelter.

"See?" I say to Kylee after we've dashed back to the car. (Madame Fidelio's nostrils flare in this awful angry way if anyone isn't standing at the barre at exactly four o'clock on the dot.) "Do I have good ideas or what?"

Seat belt buckled, Kylee reaches over and squeezes my hand. Already she's studying the first pattern in the folder. The photograph shows a poodle wearing a sweater with blue and yellow zigzag stripes.

"Some of your ideas are better than others," Kylee says. "But *this* idea is going to be great."

8

Cameron didn't notice my existence in class on Tuesday, Wednesday, or Thursday. I felt so horrible after Hunter said that Cameron thinks my poetry sucks that I pretended he didn't exist, too. But now it's Friday, and one way or another I have to find out where I stand with him, both as a poet and as a girl who is in love with him.

I still haven't heard from *The New Yorker*, even though I check my phone constantly just in case. I wonder if Ms. Archer ever sent any of her poems there. I'd love to ask her, but it's hard to find time to talk to her before or after class given that we have a four-minute passing period. While we sometimes get an opportunity to conference with her during class, that hasn't happened this week. Besides, I hate the thought that Olivia might overhear my talking to her about trying to get my poems published. If Olivia heard me ask that, she'd probably rush hers off to *The New Yorker*, too. And the last thing I'd want is for Cameron to know that I'm trying to publish my poems about him. I don't want him to know anything until I have the poem there, in print, proof that my poems aren't sucky, and are in fact the total opposite of sucky.

Before class, I say "Hey" to Cameron, who as usual is there in his seat before I get to the room; he comes from first-period language arts, right next door.

To say that one word I have to screw my courage to the sticking place, as Shakespeare said. We did a couple of scenes from Shakespeare plays in the drama camp Kylee and I signed up for this past summer, which is where I learned how bad an actress she is. I may be a better actress than Kylee is, but not good enough to say "Hey" to Cameron without feeling my cheeks flame.

"Hey," he says back, though maybe it's more of a cross between a word and a grunt.

"What are you going to write your personal essay about?" I blurt out.

He shrugs. It doesn't seem to be a rude shrug, more of an I-don't-know-yet shrug.

"You?" he asks then.

Now this is turning into an actual conversation, the kind where both people talk.

"I don't know either," I say. "I think I might write something about my br—"

How could I be such a babbling idiot? I *had* planned to take my Mrs. Whistlepuff freewrite and turn it into a full-fledged essay. But the last thing I want to talk about with Cameron is brothers, especially brothers who tease younger sisters about certain poems written about certain boys.

"Your brother." Cameron finishes the word for me, not that it's hard to figure out what word starts with "br."

I feel my ears reddening to match my already red cheeks.

"Hunter," Cameron says, as if to confirm which brother I'm talking about. "You have my condolences."

Another thing that makes Cameron seem different from the rest of us is that even in ordinary conversation he uses words most kids don't use. "You have my condolences" means that Cameron is expressing sympathy toward me for having Hunter as a brother. What it really seems to mean is that Cameron thinks Hunter is a jerk.

Why does he think Hunter is a jerk? Is Hunter a jerk because of reading my poem to the band? After all, Cameron's brother was the one who told Hunter to give my notebook back to me. So does Cameron think Hunter was mean then, too? Mean because my poem was so embarrassingly bad nobody should ever read it aloud to anyone else? Or mean because my poem was so amazingly good that nobody should ever make fun of it?

I've come to another sticking place where I need to screw more courage and force out one more syllable.

"Why?" I ask.

Cameron gives me a smile that can only be described as inscrutable, which means "impossible to understand or interpret."

"You know why," he says.

He smiles again, and this time it's not a mocking smile, exactly, but sort of an amused smile. Like the smile of a boy who knows that the girl sitting next to him wrote him a love poem. I can't tell if the smile means that he thought the love poem was good or bad. There's a limit to what you can decipher from one single smile.

Now my face must be redder than red. It's aubergine: the deep, black-purple of an eggplant.

I still don't know what Cameron thought about my poem, but that he thinks my brother is awful for making fun of it suggests that Cameron *gets* it, that he's on my side. Maybe in a romantic, protective kind of way?

Kylee slips into her seat, nearly tardy as always. Olivia

turns around to glare at Kylee for grazing her shoulder as she dashed past.

I try to think of something else to say. "Hunter didn't use to be like this."

Cameron cocks his eyebrow—like, *Yeah, right*, but also like he's interested in hearing more, as in interested in *my* brother, and so, according to the principle of transitivity we learned about in pre-algebra, interested in *me*.

"So what happened?" Cameron asks.

I'm about to say, *I think he might have changed when he joined the band.* Maybe Cameron would say that his brother changed when he joined the band, too. Maybe there's something about being in a rock band that makes older brothers start acting mean to their younger siblings. But Cameron offered me condolences about having Hunter as a brother in a way that made it sound as if my brother was a lot worse than his, if his is even bad at all.

But just then Ms. Archer calls the class to order: "Good morning, intrepid scholars." That's what she calls us sometimes, which could come off as sounding sarcastic but doesn't when she says it. "Intrepid" means bold and fearless, exactly what I want to be as a writer.

Now that class is beginning, I couldn't answer Cameron's question even if I knew the answer, which I don't. The band thing was only a guess, and maybe not a good one at that.

I wish I did know.

If I knew what happened to make Hunter change, maybe I'd know what to say or do to make him change back again.

9

On Saturday morning—well, what's left of Saturday morning (the clock on the microwave reads 11:40)—I'm in the kitchen, chatting with Mom at the table, and Hunter has just staggered downstairs—bare-chested, pj bottoms, hair looking like he mussed it on purpose to look more like a wannabe rock star, which maybe he did.

I've been up since seven-thirty. Mom says it's bad for your circadian rhythms—that's what she calls them—to sleep more than an hour later on the weekends than you do during the week. I'm a morning person anyway, so I've already showered, made French toast for me and our parents (it's the only thing I can cook, but it's delicious), knocked off a pre-algebra problem set, worked on my personal essay about Hunter, and helped Dad rake leaves.

Okay, I admit it, I'm feeling smug, and even smugger

now that Hunter has appeared half-asleep with nothing to show for his Saturday morning. Like the "Goofus and Gallant" comics I still read for old times' sake in the *Highlights* magazines at Dad's office. Goofus always does the bad thing, like leaving his dirty dishes on the table, and Gallant always does the good thing, like carrying his dirty dishes to the sink. The comic has the least subtle moral of anything in the world, but maybe I like it for that reason. With "Goofus and Gallant," you always know exactly how you're supposed to be.

Be like Gallant.

Don't be like Goofus.

In my house, though our parents would never come right out and say this, I'm clearly the family's Gallant and Hunter is the family's Goofus.

Be like Autumn.

Don't be like Hunter.

Even back in the Mrs. Whistlepuff days, I remember how Mom's forehead would furrow when Hunter would bring home his Friday folder and she'd see work that was unfinished or sloppy, with comments like "Hunter needs to check his work more carefully," "Hunter needs to learn to follow rules," and "Hunter needs to stay on task."

Our parents, being our parents, had him tested. But I

never heard anybody say he has attention-deficit disorder (ADD) or any other official thing that has a bunch of initials ending in a "D." He was just the kind of kid who couldn't sit still, who had to be drumming on the table or sassing a teacher because he thought up something super funny to say. I know our parents hoped that he'd "grow out of it." I heard Mom tell Dad once that Hunter was a "late bloomer," as if that was a fine thing to be. Daffodils bloom in the spring. Chrysanthemums bloom in the fall. It's not a *bad* thing to be a chrysanthemum.

I know they had hoped the blooming would start by the time he got to high school, but I didn't notice a whole lot of blooming going on last year. And this year—well, this year so far is a hundred times worse.

Because here's the thing about Hunter: however bad his Friday folder was, however worried Mom looked on parent-teacher-conference night, he was always nice to us. He had this great grin he'd flash after Mom or Dad yelled at him, a grin that was like, *Say whatever you want, but I know you love me anyway.*

That's what's different now.

Without even a flicker of acknowledgment, Hunter opens the fridge, grabs the carton of orange juice, and takes a swig.

"Hunter," Mom says, the scolding tone on automatic pilot, without any real energy in it.

"What?" Hunter asks, as if she hasn't told him ten thousand times to use a glass.

I see Mom's eyes roam over to the microwave clock. "You didn't use to sleep till noon. What's going on? I heard you come in at eleven"—that's Hunter's curfew on weekends, which is plenty late if you ask me—"so I know you weren't out until all hours. Did you stay up late on the computer?"

Hunter puts a piece of bread in the toaster, which surprises me. He isn't usually willing to go to that much trouble. Given the hour, maybe the piece of toast is his brunch.

"Hunter, I'm talking to you."

As if he could think she was talking to me.

"Are you having trouble sleeping?" Her tone is softer now.

I know she wishes that Hunter's new awfulness—what she likes to call his moodiness—has a simple biological explanation. It's not that Hunter has turned nasty and mean; it's that he's sleep-deprived, poor thing. Sometimes I've heard her say "Hormones" to Dad when Hunter slams a door. She says the same thing when I get extra crabby, or tear up over a B– on a paper for multicultural history. (Mr. Morton loves to give even his top students little "wake-up calls" when he thinks we're not doing our best work.)

Hunter still makes no reply.

His toast pops up.

Without even buttering it, not to mention putting it on an actual plate, he starts to walk back upstairs, toast in hand.

"Hunter James Granger!"

Don't parents know how clichéd it is to call your kids by all three names when you're extra irritated with them?

Hunter does turn around, his mouth conveniently full of toast. So maybe the three-name thing survives as part of the parenting script because it works.

"Hunter," Mom says tentatively. "Do any of the guys in the band use *drugs*? I know that musicians, well, sometimes they walk on the wild side . . . and the other band members, they're older—"

Hunter bursts out laughing. The crumbs of toast spraying out of his mouth do nothing to make his shirtless, mussed-hair, vacant-eyed look any more attractive.

"I know pot—weed—is legal in Colorado now," Mom says, unwilling to back down, "but it's not legal for anyone under twenty-one, and just as with alcohol, there are reasons why certain substances are not available to minors, whose brains and bodies are still growing and developing."

"Pot?" Hunter asks. *"Weed?"*

"Marijuana," she explains.

I know Hunter knows what pot and weed are; it's just so weird to hear Mom say the words, as if she's showing off how hip and cool she is.

For a second Hunter catches my eye and comes close to grinning at me. I almost expect him to say *Mo-o-o-m!* like when we were younger and she'd snap her fingers to music on the car radio as if that were a cool instead of pathetically uncool thing to do.

His grin vanishes before it has a chance to happen.

"Mom, I'm not using *drugs*. None of my friends are using *drugs*. Because I sleep late on a *Saturday* does not mean I'm using *drugs*. Because I'm in a *rock* band does not mean I'm using *drugs*. Because you're not in love with my *grades* doesn't mean I'm using *drugs*."

"But . . . if you were . . . I wouldn't be angry, I promise I wouldn't. I'd want you to be able to tell me, so I could get you help."

Hunter stares at her. I know he's thinking: *In what universe does a fifteen-year-old tell his mom he's smoked a few joints or had a couple of beers so she can get him* help?

"Don't worry," Hunter says, his eyes narrowing with

what looks less like anger than hatred. Anger is hot; the look on his face is icy, as if any love he ever had for any of us is frozen solid beneath the groaning weight of an Ice Age glacier. "When I need your help, I'll let you know."

He heads back upstairs, turning away before he can see Mom's face crumple into tears.

"Mom, don't," I say.

She wipes her hand across her eyes.

"I can't help remembering," she says in a voice so low I can hardly hear it, "how I'd drop him off at preschool—how he'd cry and cling to my leg and say, 'Mom, don't go.'"

What am I supposed to say?

"Well, teens are supposed to grow away from their parents," I try. "Like that pamphlet you brought home?" Yes, I read "Surviving the Teen Years: A Guide for Parents," too. I'll read anything if it's lying around and there's no other reading material handy. "And you know, hormones . . ."

"I just remember," she says, as if I hadn't spoken, "how he used to *like* me."

I was having a good day until Hunter made his brunch appearance, and now I'm having a bad day. That look of hatred was directed not just at my mother but at me, too.

Sometimes I think he hates me most of all, even though all I've ever done to him—truly all I've ever done—is to get better grades than he does and do the things our parents want us to do, like playing the flute or sticking with ballet. I can't help that I like playing the flute. I can't help that I like—well, don't really mind—doing ballet.

Dr. Jackson, my principal back in elementary school, used to say the same thing every single day at the end of morning announcements: "Have a good day—or not. The choice is yours."

Dr. Jackson obviously didn't have Hunter as her brother.

Still, I'm not going to let Hunter ruin a perfect October Saturday any more than he has already.

I text Kylee: **Bike ride by the reservoir?**

She texts back: **Can't. Knitting. Come over here?**

Now I have to decide if I want to spend a crisp, cool, cloudless autumn day watching someone else knit dog sweaters. I decide I don't. Kylee hasn't put down her needles since she got that folder of patterns and bag of yarn at the animal shelter. I've created a knitting monster.

Brianna is away visiting her grandparents, and Isabelle has some kind of maybe-flu thing I don't want to catch. So I'll just curl up and be a writing monster. I'm not going to write any more poetry until I hear from *The New Yorker*, so I go back to my novel. I need to get rid of the finding-the-amulet scene in the Tatiana and Ingvar book and launch Tatiana on her next harrowing adventure.

Dad comes into the kitchen before I can make my get-away. One look at Mom's blotchy face, and the muscles in his jaw twitch. Dad can handle just about anything Hunter and I do so long as we're not mean to Mom.

"What did he say this time, Suzanne?" Dad asks.

"Oh, nothing really," Mom replies. "The usual."

"The usual," Dad repeats. I know it makes things worse that how Hunter acts isn't even surprising anymore, just how he *is*. Dad forces a smile. "Autumn, do your mother and me a favor and always stay as sweet a kid as you are today."

I don't think of myself as particularly sweet, but maybe on a sweetness scale of 1 to 10, a kid who makes French toast for her parents and helps her dad rake leaves without being asked would score at least an 8.

"What do we have going on this afternoon?" Dad asks Mom.

"I promised Hunter I'd take him out driving."

Dad shakes his head, not overruling her, but more like he's perplexed by the whole Hunter situation. "Maybe someone needs to learn that 'the usual' isn't the way you earn time behind the wheel."

"Things will be better when he gets his license," she says.

Why on earth would Mom think that?

"If he has more independence, more autonomy, maybe he won't need to say and do things that are . . . you know . . . so hurtful. Anyway, I promised, and I like to keep my promises if possible, and he really wasn't *that* rude or disrespectful."

Dad cocks his eyebrow the way he does when Mom goes into her protective Mama Bear routine.

She continues, "And tomorrow he's practicing with the band for most of the day at Timber's. They have a gig in two weeks!"

Now Dad really looks bewildered. I don't think he had thought of Hunter's band as a real band, the kind of band that real people would ask to play in real places. It's the first I've heard about the gig, too.

"Where?" is all he says, but I can hear that he wants to say *On what planet?*

"The Spotted Cow coffee shop in the strip mall where the Chinese restaurant is," she says. "I don't think they've been hired, exactly. It's more the kind of thing where you just show up and play."

"Okay," Dad says. "That makes more sense."

I feel a twinge of pity for Hunter. What Dad said was hardly terrible, but it's clear from what he didn't say that he thinks the band—which is the only thing in the world Hunter seems to care about right now—is a hopeless cause.

Even though Hunter has been nonstop mean to me for weeks now, I'm glad the band has a gig. I really am.

10

Our personal essays are due on Friday. In journalism class on Monday, Ms. Archer hands out copies of a couple of published personal essays that she thinks are models of everything a personal essay should be. One of them is about the day someone realized that she was more racist than she had thought she was. It made me squirm, in a good way, because the author was willing to be so honest about something bad about herself. I'm not so good at owning up to my faults. The other essay is light and funny until the very end, when it stabs you in the heart. The author's cat does all these hilarious and ridiculous things but then goes outside one day and never comes back.

"What's this one about?" Ms. Archer asks, after she finishes reading the cat essay out loud to us.

I'm not sure. I think it's about how it's worth it to be

fully alive, even if there are risks involved. But I stay a quiet lurker.

"Cameron?" Ms. Archer asks, even though, as far as I can tell, Cameron hasn't given any signal that he has something to say. He's still just doodling, doodling, doodling.

He answers without looking up. "It's better to go outside and get hit by a car than to live your life trapped inside. It's better to die all at once, not by inches."

I love his answer. I love that it's what I was going to say, only in different words. Now I wish I had raised my hand, so he'd know that he and I thought the same thing.

"All right," Ms. Archer says, once we've talked more about the two sample essays, with Olivia raising her hand four times to offer her insights about their structure. "Let's do another freewrite. Disregard everything we said in analyzing these two pieces to death"—is that a jab at Olivia? Oh, I hope it is!—"and write your little hearts out. Here's your prompt for the next few minutes: something you don't like about yourself."

I should have known she'd do that one, given that I had just been thinking how I don't like writing bad things about myself. Especially when I'm sitting next to Cameron and he might look over and see what I'm writing, not that he's ever given any sign of interest in me—well, until our last conversation about Hunter.

So I sit there paralyzed.

What don't I like about myself?

My flat chest. As if I'm going to write about that!

Being too tall. It's pitiful to care about something so trivial.

Okay. Maybe what I don't like about myself is that I do care about a lot of shallow, pitiful things. I do care too much about what other people think about me. When you get right down to it, my get-published-soon plan is about impressing other people, especially other people named Cameron and Hunter and Olivia. But what's the point of being a writer if you're not going to try to connect with a reader, preferably with lots of readers? The authors who wrote the racism essay and the cat essay—didn't they care about being read by other human beings? If they didn't, why did they have their essays published rather than leaving them in a drawer? Most writers are not like Emily Dickinson.

Then I see that Cameron has written something: something very short, in the far corner of his blank page. It looks like a haiku.

I roll my shoulders and rotate my head as if I'm doing some physical therapy exercise to help with writer's block, holding the pose for an extra second as I strain to read what Cameron has written. But his writing is sort of like calligraphy, with fancy little flourishes that make it hard to decipher, especially if you're pretending not to be trying to read it in the first place.

Then Cameron turns his paper toward me.

I feel myself flushing scarlet. He must think that's just the color I am all the time: beet red.

I could try to act puzzled—*Oh, wait, did you think I was looking at your paper?*—but there's really no point to that now. So I just read what he's written.

I can't see myself
Only what the mirror shows
But all mirrors lie

I love it.

If *The New Yorker* published haiku—and I didn't see any haiku there either—they would definitely publish this. It's so deep and wise and true. It takes the whole "what don't you like about yourself" prompt and turns it inside out. How can we know what we like or don't like about ourselves, when we can't even see ourselves, we can only see what the mirror shows? And what Cameron wrote connects with what I didn't write, about how I care too much about what other people think.

I can't help smiling at Cameron.

"It's beautiful," I whisper.

Cameron doesn't return my smile or acknowledge my praise. He starts doodling all over the rest of the page and keeps on doodling. And for the first time this trimester, I don't write anything either. Instead I just sit and chant Cameron's haiku over and over again to myself.

Then in the last minute of class, I write a mirror haiku of my own:

No mirror shows me
An image more real and true
Than one that is cracked.

I can't help myself: just before the bell is about to ring, I turn my paper so Cameron can see it.

As I suck in my breath, he reads it and gives a curt nod. Of approval? Or just acknowledgment?

I like his haiku better than mine. But I like mine, too. I think it's deep. I think it's even *profound*. I like that we wrote them, side by side, together, on the same day.

11

Ms. Archer gives us class time to work on our personal essays on Thursday. Kylee lets me read what she's done on hers so far. It's about knitting—surprise, surprise. It's about how she learned to knit, taught by her Chinese grandmother, who died earlier this year.

Kylee is half Chinese (her mother) and half not Chinese (her father). Some kids and even some teachers expect Kylee to be a math-and-science whiz because she's part Asian, but she's not at all mathematical or scientific, and neither is her mom. Kylee says that's a stereotype, and even though it's a positive stereotype and not a negative one, it's just as annoying.

Her essay is good. It's sweet and touching and really sensory. You can feel the warmth of the tea she's drinking as she knits, and how it's a metaphor for the warmth of the relationship she had with her grandmother.

But is it *about* something? Or is it just an incident?

Right now my piece about Hunter and Mrs. Whistle-puff feels like an incident, too: here's a nice thing my brother once did for me. Mine is even more of an incident than Kylee's. You could say that hers is about the value of passing on family traditions, about how little things like knitting together can feel so big when someone is gone and only the memory remains. Kylee's piece starts with the line "Po Po died last May." That lets us know right from the start the essay is going to be about surviving loss.

Now that I think of it, my piece is about the exact same thing. The person I loved is gone, like Kylee's grandmother, but in a different way. My piece is about surviving loss, too, about how people who once loved you may not love you anymore, but you still love them because of things they did back when they did love you. Though right now I have to admit I don't feel a whole lot of love for Hunter, just this sickening kind of hurt inside me.

But I don't think any of this comes through now, the way I've written it.

I gather up my essay and my writing notebook to take them over to Ms. Archer's desk. One of the reasons she gives us in-class writing time is so that we can conference with her as much as we need to.

Olivia is already talking to her, of course, leaning forward in the conference chair, tossing her long dark hair as she gestures animatedly. Olivia talks one-on-one to Ms. Archer every single in-class-writing day. I guess she's entitled to. Half the time Ms. Archer is sitting there waiting for someone to talk to her, so it isn't as if Olivia is taking time away from anyone else. But it makes her seem needy or greedy, soooo eager to be the teacher's pet. I know, I know. I shouldn't think such hateful things about Olivia, because down deep—well, not down all that deep—I'm as needy and greedy and teacher's pet-y as she is.

When Olivia is done—she used up seven whole minutes—I plunk myself down in the chair next to Ms. Archer's desk. Wordlessly I hand her my essay. I added some stuff to it since the freewrite. I put in some of the other things I was—am—afraid of, like spiders and eyeballs (if I ever need glasses, I'm never getting contact lenses) and chairlifts where your feet hang down. At the end I added the thought about how I don't have the flashlight anymore, just the memory. Other than that, though, it's pretty much the same.

It's the tensest moment in a writer's life: to sit there watching someone reading what you've written. The only thing even tenser is if they're reading something you've written about your *life*.

Ms. Archer isn't reading fast or slow, and she doesn't show any reaction. I can't stop my eyes from trying to read upside down, so I can be reading exactly what she's reading, exactly when she's reading it.

She looks up when she's done and smiles.

"This is lovely, Autumn. So many vivid details to let the reader experience a five-year-old's fear. Even as we know there is no such person as Mrs. Whistlepuff, you've made us believe in her. You've done a deft job of showing the family dynamics with so few words: 'my father took the night-light out of my room because five-year-olds are big girls who don't need night-lights anymore.' And you've made us love Hunter."

Ms. Archer always starts with the positive. That's good, but it makes me wonder if she means the nice things she says, because she really does find something nice to say to everyone.

"But?" I ask, prompting her for the criticism I know is coming.

"What do *you* think it needs?" She turns the question back at me.

"It's just an incident? It's not *about* anything?"

She considers this. "It's about overcoming fear?" she suggests. "And how sometimes, as Beatle Ringo Starr once sang, 'we get by with a little help from our friends'? How could you bring out that idea a bit more?"

I shake my head. That's *not* what it's about, not for me.

"Or?" she asks.

"It's about my brother. How he used to be. Versus how he is now . . ."

Even as I say it, I know this is not the right kind of about-ness. About-ness isn't supposed to be personal; it's the universal truth you're trying to share with the reader. That's what Ms. Archer told us the day we did the best-or-worst-present freewrite.

I'm so tuned in to Ms. Archer that when she gives a slight nod, I know she's not nodding for what I said, but for the ellipsis points at the end of it, for how I realized myself that it wasn't enough.

"Actually," I say miserably, "I don't think it's about anything that anybody except me would care about."

That's why I came to you. Tell me what it should be about. Tell me how to fix it. Tell me what the universal truth is supposed to be.

"Maybe . . ." she says.

Tell me, tell me, tell me!

86

"Maybe you're not ready to write this yet. Let it simmer. Let it stew."

It's due tomorrow!

"What it means will come to you," she continues. "You'll wake up in the middle of the night someday, some month, some year, and say, 'Cumin!' or 'Coriander!'"

I don't cook, except for my killer French toast, but I recognize those as names of spices. My essay needs more than a spice. It needs the central ingredient. Right now it's like chicken soup without the chicken.

"But now I see," Ms. Archer says. "I was wrong before. Take out the bits about the spiders and the chairlift. Those are red herrings. They lead us in the wrong direction."

Isn't that always the way it is when you write? She wants me to take out the very things I worked so hard to add in.

"This isn't about fear," she says as she hands my essay back to me. "It's about love."

12

I end up writing my personal essay on something entirely different. Well, maybe not *entirely* different. I write about "Goofus and Gallant," and how hard I tried to be like Gallant when I was little, but how now I feel kind of sorry for Goofus and sick and tired of Gallant, too.

I write it late that night, after the band concert, where my flute solo went *great* and Hunter wasn't there to hear it, claiming he had too much homework. Mom and Dad let him get away with not coming because they're so desperate to believe Hunter actually cares about homework and is actually doing any of it.

The essay is definitely *about* something. It's about how people aren't all bad or good, how the lines between bad and good get blurred all the time, and how that's a good thing.

But I think I spelled the point out too clearly.

When we hand them in on Friday, I want to ask Cameron what he wrote about, but I don't want to sound like a total stalker girl. I do peer over at his desk as casually as I can so that I can read the first line: *My mother says the first thing I ever loved was rocks.*

In my view, that is a wonderful first line.

Does he still love rocks? Rocks are sort of a strange thing to love. But one of the things I love best about Cameron is that he's not afraid to be strange.

As she collects our essays, Ms. Archer says, "I can't wait to read these!" I hope she likes mine, whether I spelled out the point too clearly or not.

When she has them in a tidy pile on her desk, she holds up a flyer. "Breaking news: This was in my mailbox this morning, an announcement of a contest for, yes, personal essays! From the *Denver Post*. And—this is the best part— the contest is for essays from young writers ages twelve to sixteen. In other words, writers like you."

The deadline for the contest is one week from today, Friday, October 21. They'll let the winners know by mid-November. Winners will get their work published on the op-ed page of the newspaper—that's the page *op*posite the *edi*torial page.

Ms. Archer says we have to submit the essays ourselves,

only one essay per applicant. I copy down the website address she gives us. Olivia copies it down, too, of course. Cameron doesn't. Kylee doesn't either.

I have my "Goofus and Gallant" essay completely done, so I could send it off today as soon as I get home from school. But maybe I should wait first to see what grade Ms. Archer gives it. If I can only send in one essay, I want to make sure the one I send is my very best. I don't think this one is as good as the essay I started about Mrs. Whistlepuff, the one I didn't know how to finish. So maybe I should try to finish that one instead.

But how?

That's what I need to figure out. Because it's hard not to feel that this contest flyer, showing up in Ms. Archer's mailbox at this very moment, is a sign from the universe for me.

A sign for me, not for Olivia.

The band comes over to practice at our house again on Saturday afternoon. This time I do not change into a flowing, poetic-looking dress for possible admiration by observant older brothers. What I *should* do is stay in my room as far away from the band as possible or, better still, go to Kylee's house and watch her knit. I could also text Brianna and Isabelle to see if they are free, but lately all they want to talk about is the Southern Peaks seventh- and eighth-grade fall dance, which is a whole month away. Mostly, though, I don't text anybody because I just want to be where the band is in case David says anything about me to Hunter, or Hunter says anything about me to David. I can't help myself, but I do.

Before they arrive, I grab my Moleskine notebook, to make sure that it's not out of my possession for one single solitary second. The couches in the family room aren't right against the walls; my mother thinks they're more "inviting" if they're positioned at an angle. So there's space for me to hide behind one of them, cozy on the carpet between the back of the couch and the bookcase, where nobody can find me, for who's going to go looking for a book during a band practice? I bring a couple of pillows from the couch with me to make it more comfortable.

This time the guys hang out in the family room first, rather than the kitchen, before heading downstairs. Mom is baking brownies for them—not healthy brownies either, but her great oozy-fudgy kind—and they aren't quite out of the oven yet.

They talk about the gig, the gig, the gig, which is a week from today. It's so boring I tune out their conversation and tune in thoughts about my Mrs. Whistlepuff essay. What can I add to make its larger significance more clear?

But then another Hunter memory comes to me, a much more recent one, and it all seems to connect somehow, and my hand flies across the page as if my brain isn't even doing the writing. It's like I hear this voice in my head dictating the words to me, this voice in my head urging me, *Write this down.*

I'm twelve now, and Hunter is fifteen. Mrs. Whistle-puff is gone forever. But the brother I loved is gone, too. He still sleeps in our house and eats at our table. But he's mean to me all the time, and I don't know why.

One day last summer Hunter was off at cross-country practice—our dad made him go. It was so hot the tar in the asphalt in the driveway was bubbling. It was so hot there was a power outage in our subdivision because the AC in everybody's houses had to work too hard.

My brother came home from practice at five. His hair, which is longer than it used to be, dripped with sweat. His face was streaked with dirt.

Dad said, "Hunter, I'm proud of you for sticking it out on this hottest of days."

Hunter said, "I'm not sticking it out. I quit."

Dad said, "What do you mean, you quit? You made a commitment!"

Hunter said, "You made the commitment, not me."

Then Dad stalked out of the room with this look of total disgust on his face. As long as I live, I hope nobody ever looks at me that way, especially nobody in my family. Though, actually, that's exactly the way Hunter sometimes looks at me these days.

I thought Hunter might run after him and say, Dad, I changed my mind. I'll stick it out. Really, I will.

He didn't. He just stood there looking as furious as I've ever seen a person look, like he had a dragon inside belching flames as scorching hot as Mrs. Whistlepuff's breath was freezing cold.

But he also looked like he was going to cry tears as scalding as Mrs. Whistlepuff's breath was icy.

If I still had that flashlight, I'd give it to him to scare away that dragon. Or maybe I'm the one who needs to have that flashlight to scare away Hunter's dragon when it breathes fire at me.

But I don't have it. Or at least I can't find it.

I don't know if I'll ever be able to find it again.

I'm writing so intently that I'm only jarred back into consciousness of the band's presence by hearing Cameron's name.

What did I just miss?

"I brought another song of his. I think this one's good enough for us to play at the gig," David says.

I try to piece the conversation together. So Cameron does write songs. And the band is going to play one! Now I'll have to perch at the top of the basement stairs when they finally head down and listen to the practice to try to figure out which song is his. I don't dare to hope the song Cameron wrote for the band is about me. No, it couldn't be.

But what if it is?

They're back to talking about playing a tune from some band I never heard of, and then they're tromping down the stairs making almost as much noise with their feet as they're about to make with their music.

I'm getting ready to escape from my hiding place, which is feeling more cramped by the minute, when Hunter reappears in the room, calling downstairs to the others, "I'll just be a sec. There's a record I want you to hear."

Hunter is totally into vinyl these days. He saved a bunch

of Dad's old records when Mom was going to donate them to Goodwill in one of her decluttering fits.

Then it registers.

The records are on the bottom shelf of the bookcase.

The bookcase where I'm hiding.

This is when I wish I had Tatiana's magic wand, captured from Ingvar, to make myself invisible, or her amulet to ward off danger.

But I don't.

His eyes widen when he sees me. "What the—"

"I was just writing," I say, holding up my notebook as proof, at the same time that I'm clutching it to my chest in case he makes a snatch for it.

"You were just *spying*," he says.

Well, what if I was? A person is allowed to spy on somebody who might be making fun of her to somebody else who is the brother of the person she is in love with. Right?

"As if I'd want to spy on you and your dumb friends," I say with as much haughtiness as I can muster.

Hunter's face registers new understanding.

"You were spying on *David*," he says. "Give it up, Autumn. Like you'd ever have a chance with Cameron. The stuff he writes is actually good. Unlike a certain so-called *poet*." In a warbling falsetto, he begins a screeching tune,

"Oh, Cam-er-on! I love theeeee!" He's clearly doing his best to sound like a dying cat.

"Hunter!" one of the guys bellows from the basement. "Are you coming or what?"

Hunter grabs one of the records and disappears without another word. Which is lucky for him, as my eyes are glittering with tears of a fury so pure and poisonous one drop could kill him dead.

I'm back upstairs in my room, with the door slammed shut. If only I had a lock! But Mom doesn't believe in locks on bedroom doors. Hunter wanted to get one last month, and she said, "Family members don't lock their doors against other family members." But I'm locking my heart against Hunter right now.

It's been a whole two hours since I checked the emails on my phone, probably the longest ever since I sent my poems to *The New Yorker* almost two weeks ago.

When I check my phone now, my inbox has one new message.

It's from *The New Yorker*.

It's been nowhere near two to six months. Maybe they love my poems so much they have to publish one of them right away? Maybe they hate my poems so much they have to reject all of them right away? The editor sent the email on a Saturday. Do all editors work on weekends? Or was this editor just so excited by my poems he couldn't wait until Monday to let me know?

Before I let myself read the message, I stare at the sender's address for one long moment: my first email from *The New Yorker*.

How many writers my age are even getting emails from *The New Yorker*?

Then I read it.

My poems don't suit their "current publishing needs."

That's all they say.

I didn't realize how much I'd been counting on a yes from *The New Yorker* until now, when I'm staring down at my phone and rereading that message over and over again. For the past two weeks, every day was a little more special, knowing that this was the day I might hear the news that my Cameron poems would be published in the most prestigious poetry magazine that there is.

I try to tell myself, *Okay,* The New Yorker *didn't like my poems. Frankly, I don't like their poems either.* I knew it was a long shot, trying to publish rhyming love poems nowadays. Like Miniver Cheevy and Moonbeam, I was born too late.

But the more I read over that one short line, the more it hurts. Couldn't they have said *something* encouraging? Commented on my promise as a poet and suggested that I might consider branching out a bit and writing poems that don't rhyme? Asked me to try them again with other material?

I click on the file I sent them and read through my six rhyming Cameron poems, trying to imagine an editor sitting in a faraway New York City office coming upon them amid thousands of other poems sent in by other wannabe poets.

Is Hunter right that they suck? Or is Hunter wrong?

Did Cameron tell David he hated my poem? Or did Hunter make that up?

Right now it feels like Hunter was right, about everything.

I don't plan to cry.

But somehow that's what I'm doing as I imagine the *New Yorker* editor reading my poor little rejected poems aloud to the guy sitting next to him, borrowing Hunter's quavery falsetto voice, and the other guy laughing for a brief moment before cheerfully going on to reject the next poem, and the next poem, and the poem after that.

13

On Monday Ms. Archer hands back our personal essays.

I get an A on mine. Maybe the A is partly because I had to put the Mrs. Whistlepuff essay aside at the last minute and start all over again, an A for effort. But it doesn't really matter because I already sent my expanded Mrs. Whistle-puff essay to the *Denver Post* contest last night. I couldn't sleep, thinking about Hunter's meanness and the *New Yorker* rejection. So at two in the morning I slipped out of bed, turned on my computer, and did the deed.

Kylee got an A on her essay, too. I don't know what Cameron got on his. I do know he stuck it inside his journalism binder without even looking at it. (Ms. Archer hands them back to us facedown, to protect each student's privacy from prying eyes—like mine.)

"All right, intrepid scholars," Ms. Archer says. "Next

up, we'll be spending two weeks reading and writing reviews."

"Reviews of what?" Tyler wants to know. "Video games?" he asks hopefully.

"Of anything!" Ms. Archer replies. "Video games, books, films, plays, restaurants, shops, services. Anything where you think your opinion might be helpful to someone trying to decide whether to purchase or attend or engage with that thing."

As soon as she said "books," I thought about the book I love best and would most want to tell the world about: *Wuthering Heights* by Emily Brontë. But most people already know about that book. Shouldn't the review be about something *new*? I feel too shy to ask.

"A review, say, of a book"—Ms. Archer must be reading my mind—"must be more than just a summary of the plot, though you do want to give the reader a sense of what the story is about, while avoiding spoilers that would destroy the reading experience. Above all, the reader wants *your* opinion about the plot, the characters, the theme, the writing style. But a review also needs to be more than just your *opinion*: I loved this, I hated that. Your opinion needs to be supported with details and examples. *Why* did you love this? *Why* did you hate that?"

Tyler calls out another question. "What if you hate the whole thing?"

Ms. Archer laughs. "It's true that reviews make a stronger impression if they take a bold stance rather than being timid or wishy-washy. But you also want to be fair. Readers want to be able to trust your judgment as being impartial rather than biased."

Olivia raises her hand. "Is anybody going to be *reading* these reviews?" she asks. "Except for you, of course? And other kids in the class?"

"I'm glad you asked," Ms. Archer says. "One appealing feature of review writing is how easy it is to publish reviews online these days, on sites like Goodreads, for books, or Amazon, for just about anything, or on a business's own website. But the ease of posting your review doesn't mean you should compromise your standards as writers. You wouldn't want to post anything on which you wouldn't be proud to sign your name."

It would be fun to post a review online. But I don't think a review posted on a website would count as a real publication.

"I'll also be evaluating your reviews," Ms. Archer continues, "to see if any of them might be right for the *Peaks Post*."

The *Peaks Post* is the Southern Peaks Middle School paper. Ms. Archer is the adviser for it, as well as our journalism teacher. The editors for the paper are eighth graders who already took the journalism class last year; regular school events are covered by students who signed up to be staff writers. I haven't done that, maybe because Hunter calls it the *Pukes Post*. Anyone can submit features, reviews, or op-eds to the paper at any time. Then the byline reads "Special to the *Peaks Post.*" Sometimes articles in the *Peaks Post* are picked up by the grown-up paper in town, the *Broomville Banner*, which would be a pretty amazing thing to have happen.

Now I definitely need to think of something to review other than *Wuthering Heights*. There is no way that either the *Peaks Post* or the *Broomville Banner* would want to publish a review of a book written centuries ago.

Ms. Archer gives a smile that seems to say she's sure she's going to find at least one publishable review from someone in our class. Then she says, "I'm going to give you a few minutes to brainstorm ideas for what you might want to review with the people sitting near you. Try to think of something where you might have special expertise that could inform your evaluation. Or something unusual that others might not think of reviewing."

I'm sitting next to Cameron, of course, and Kylee is

on my other side. Olivia, Kaitlyn, and Tyler are right in front of us. So we pull our desks together in an awkward circle.

I wish Olivia sat on the other side of the room.

I wish Olivia weren't even in our class.

"What are the rest of you thinking about doing?" she asks. I notice she doesn't tell us first what she's planning to do. Maybe she has some idea so wonderful she wants to keep it to herself.

To my surprise, Kylee, who is usually even quieter than I am, which is saying a lot, says without a moment's hesitation, "I'm going to review Knit Wits."

Everybody else looks blank. The name sounds just like "Nitwits." Only I know that it's a new shop in the mall that has every kind of yarn on earth, made of wool not just from sheep but also from alpacas, llamas, Angora rabbits, even camels.

"It's a knitting store," Kylee explains.

Olivia rolls her eyes, but Tyler says, "Cool! If anyone knows about knitting, it's you, Kylee."

"I'm going to review the new Disney film," Kaitlyn said. "The one that's coming out this weekend."

That sounds like an extremely ordinary idea to me, but Olivia, who has somehow become the official dispenser of approval or disapproval, gives a gracious nod.

Tyler says he's going to review some video game I've never heard of. As he says it, he pantomimes his hands twitching on the controller.

"What about you, Cameron?" Olivia asks.

Cameron has been doodling the whole time, but he looks up to say, "Cosmic Eruption." When everyone looks as mystified as when Kylee mentioned Knit Wits, he says, "It's an indie band."

"Autumn?" Olivia asks.

I have an idea cosmically erupting in my brain now, but there is no way I'm going to say it in front of Olivia or Cameron; I'll save it to tell Kylee later when we're completely alone.

"Probably just a book," I mumble.

"Which book?" Olivia pursues.

I can just imagine the eye roll I'd get for saying *Wuthering Heights*.

"I haven't decided anything yet," I say.

"What about *you*?" Kaitlyn asks Olivia. "I bet you have the coolest idea of all."

Kylee and I think that sort of thing about each other—I mean, we're both each other's biggest fans—but we don't show it in front of other people to make them feel bad.

"I haven't decided anything yet either," Olivia says. Then she relents. "Well, there's a new cupcake store on Ninth Street. It would be fun to have an excuse to taste all their cupcakes."

"Oooh!" Kaitlyn squeals.

I have to admit that's a review I'd like to read or, even more, a review I'd like to write. But I already have my own idea.

My own extremely terrific idea.

Guess who is going to go to a certain gig this weekend and write a review of a certain band named Paradox?

On a five-star scale, guess how many stars I'm going to give them? I wish I could give them zero, but on the rating sites for things, one star is the lowest you can give. But it's what I'll *say* about them that matters.

In class on the very first day of the new school year, Ms. Archer told us, "The pen is mightier than the sword."

And the published pen is mightier than anything.

What if Ms. Archer chooses my review to publish in the school paper? And what if the *Broomville Banner* publishes it next? Maybe the Associated Press will pick it up! And the terrible things I'll say about Hunter's band will be read by people all over the world.

Nothing is sweeter than a writer's revenge.

"You *have* to come with me," I plead with Kylee.

I'm at her house on Saturday afternoon, in her room, sitting cross-legged on her bed, next to a growing pile of finished dog sweaters, each one cuter than the last. She told me she feels guilty she's only finished five so far, but five sounds like a lot to me. It's five more dog sweaters than most people on this planet have to show for themselves.

"I need to finish seven more by a week from Wednesday," she says.

"Why a week from Wednesday?"

"That's the deadline." Kylee's fingers click along on the needles as fast as my fingers click along on a computer keyboard. I wonder if she knows how many stitches she can knit in a minute.

"What do you mean, the deadline? Don't cold little dogs need sweaters just as much on Thursday? Or Friday? Besides, winter's still two months away."

"That's the last day of the special knit-for-dogs drive," Kylee answers.

"And why *seven* more sweaters? You act like you're an oppressed worker in some sweatshop in China."

She looks directly at me.

I shouldn't have made a joke about China.

"In some sweatshop somewhere," I correct myself. "Like if you don't meet your quota, you'll be fired and your family will starve to death."

"Donating a dozen sweaters is my personal goal." Kylee sounds like her usual placid self, to my relief after the unfortunate sweatshop-in-China comment. Yet her fingers look anything but placid as she keeps the needles click-click-clicking. "And *dogs* might *freeze* to death if I don't make them."

"The sweaters are for the *shelter* dogs," I remind her. "They're not going to round up all the stray dogs in Broomville so they can dress them up in sweaters."

"*You* have goals," Kylee says. Her tone has an un-placid edge to it now. "You want to publish your Cameron poems in *The New Yorker*."

I haven't told Kylee about the rejection yet. It's the first time ever in our friendship that I haven't told her something. I'm not quite sure why. I guess I feel not only heartbroken about it but also ashamed at how pitiful I was to dream so big and fail so badly.

"And you want to publish your review of the band in the *Peaks Post*, and the *Broomville Banner*, and someplace where everyone in the world will read it." Of course, I told her that after school on Monday. "So this is *my* goal," Kylee finishes.

I want Kylee to achieve her goal as much as she wants me to achieve mine. But how can I achieve mine if she doesn't agree to go to the gig with me tonight? I could call Brianna or Isabelle. But no one else understands how I feel about Cameron, and there's a good chance Cameron will be at the gig, since the band is playing one of his songs. I still don't know which one is his because of being too distraught to listen to the practice that day, but I'm sure I'll recognize it when I hear it. Writers show their soul in what they write.

"*Please* come?" I make my voice high and squeaky and irresistibly adorable. "Please, please, please, *please?*"

"It will be loud," Kylee says.

True.

"It will be dark."

Also probably true.

"I'll hate every minute of it."

I try to come up with some reason weighty enough to overcome her objections. "I think Cameron might be there, and . . . well . . . Just come with me. That's all I ask. You can bring your knitting with you."

Kylee tosses aside her knitting and flings herself down

on her bedspread in a gesture of surrender. Face buried in dog sweaters, she says, "This is a one-time thing. I am *not*—I repeat *not*—going to be a Paradox groupie, no matter how many songs Cameron writes for them. Agreed?"

"Agreed," I say.

I'm so relieved and grateful, there's nothing I wouldn't agree to right now.

Besides, given how scathing my review of Paradox is going to be, and how widely I plan for it to be published, this may well be the only gig the band ever has.

14

"You have got to be kidding," Dad says when I ask him at dinner if he can drive Kylee and me to the gig. The Spotted Cow is bike-riding distance from our house, but I'm not allowed to ride after dark. "You hear them play all the time right here in your own home."

Hunter isn't eating with us. He's off with the band doing a last-minute practice at Timber's house.

"Kidding?" I ask, trying not to reveal my hidden agenda. "This is different. It's Hunter's first gig!"

"All right," Dad says. "We can give you a ride. Call us when you're ready for a ride home. Hunter is lucky to have a sister who is so devoted."

His last words sting.

Hunter is *un*lucky to have a sister who is a very angry writer.

What do you wear to a gig? Kylee and I confer via text. We decide we can't go wrong with jeans, boots, and dark tops with a little sparkly neckline (Kylee) and a plain silver necklace (me). I curl my hair for the occasion. Usually I let it hang straight because I can't be bothered fussing with it.

My father doesn't notice, but my mother does.

"You look nice, sweetie," is all she says. But I know she's thinking: *Is there more to this gig than you're letting on?*

She knows a little bit about Cameron, chiefly because of Hunter's Cameron-themed insults in the car, but that's really all. Some of my friends, like Isabelle, tell their moms about every boy they have a crush on. I think Kylee would tell her mom if she did have a crush on anyone, which she doesn't. Her only crush is the one she has on her knitting needles. But I'm selective about the things I say in person to anyone but Kylee. I'm better at saying things to my notebook.

When Kylee and I arrive at the Spotted Cow, it's bigger than Dad made it sound. There are a dozen tables and a good-sized performance space with a baby grand piano in it, plus room for amps, drums, and a band. Almost all the tables are full. It takes me a few moments to let my eyes sweep over them in the low light of the café. Cameron isn't there. Neither are any of the members of Hunter's band.

Kylee and I order steamers—vanilla for her, raspberry-chocolate-hazelnut for me (I love when a barista lets me mix flavors). Steamers aren't a coffee drink; they're just warm milk with Italian soda syrups mixed in—yum. We sit at the only empty table we can find. Unfortunately, it's right next to the performance space. So much for hoping that Hunter might not even see me there. I don't want him to know about the review until it's too late to stop me.

The first band up is called the Electric Orangutans. Their five members are singing a song that sounds like a deafeningly loud chant by medieval monks wearing black jeans and black T-shirts. If it has words, rather than guttural hums, I can't make out what they are.

I take a sip of my steamer. Kylee produces her knitting from her oversized purse. A thought pops into my overheated brain (it's too warm in here, as well as too loud): Given that there are no empty tables right now, Cameron—if he comes—may need to sit at ours.

Is it okay if I join you? I imagine him saying or, rather, mouthing, since it's too loud for any words to be heard.

Or maybe he'd pantomime, pointing to the one empty chair at our small table, and then to himself, with a questioning expression on his face: *Do you mind?*

Now I almost wish I hadn't begged Kylee to come.

It would have been almost like a *date* for Cameron and me.

Except for all the ways it isn't.

Ten minutes later, the Orangutans are apparently done performing. They've started putting their instruments back in the cases and dismantling their drums so that Paradox can set up.

But where is Paradox?

Then I see them, coming in from a door in the back, the stage door, probably.

Cameron is with them. He's helping Hunter drag in the many components of his drum set: bass drum, snare drum, hi-hat cymbals. I can't believe someone as wonderful as Cameron is a roadie for someone as awful as Hunter. Maybe he doesn't think Hunter is as condolence-worthy as he led me to believe.

Kylee keeps on knitting, but her eyes meet mine. I'm definitely glad I made her come with me now. She's the only reason I can survive being here at all.

It's blissfully quiet in the Spotted Cow between sets.

The barista who made my triple-flavored steamer comes to the mike to make an announcement.

"Thanks for coming out tonight, everyone," he says, "to support live music. Our musicians aren't getting paid for their time and talent, so remember to tip generously."

He points to a large jar on top of the piano, about two feet away from Kylee and me, which has one twenty-dollar bill in it. I'm sure it was put there ahead of time to inspire customers to tip large-denomination bills rather than whatever spare change they find in their pockets.

"And now please join me in welcoming to the stage . . . Paradox!"

The audience gives a roar of applause. Kylee and I clap, too. I'm opening my Moleskine to a blank page and uncapping my pen when Cameron sits down next to me.

No mouthed request to join us, no humble chair-pointing gesture. He sits down, as if any empty chair is for the taking, including the one that happens to be at our table.

Then he smiles at me, not a huge toothy grin that lights up his face, but a sort of slow half smile, like: *We meet again.*

I might faint.

I'm still going to take notes on the concert. Maybe

Cameron will think it's cool that I'm willing to sit in public devoting myself to my art. Maybe it will look as if I don't care what anybody else thinks, just the way he doesn't care what anyone else thinks—even though I actually do care about what *he* thinks more than anything else in the world. But it's hard to anticipate what he'll think about anything.

As the band plays their first number—and I have to admit it sounds good, with a catchy melody and driving beat—I write down cleverly disparaging turns of phrase I can use in my review:

> *The real paradox is that anybody would ever voluntarily listen to this music.*
>
> *If you want a way to kill live music, this is it.*
>
> *If not dead before, the song was beaten to death by the mishandled drumsticks of incompetent drummer Hunter Granger.*
>
> *The torn T-shirts, evidently purchased from some rockstar-wannabe website, were designed to give the false impression of having been ripped by adoring fans.*
>
> *They make the error of confusing* loud *with* good.
>
> *The original artists who first recorded these songs should sue.*

Another number finishes, to whoops and hollers from the audience. Oh, well. Opinions can differ. That's why reviews are interesting to read, because not everybody thinks the same way about everything.

David, at the mike, says something, and I hear Cameron's name. He must have said either that the *last* song was by Cameron or that the *next* song would be by Cameron. Do people announce a song before or after it's played?

I was hardly listening to the song they just played, too busy thinking up witty insults. But it didn't sound as if it had come pouring out of Cameron's soul.

It has to be the next song, I decide. *Please let it be the next song.*

The tempo changes. The song is slower, softer, not music for which you'd need earplugs. I wish I had a copy of the lyrics so I could read along as David and Timber sing, but I can make out at least some of the words.

"I tell myself that I don't care . . .
But I do.
I tell myself that it's just me . . .
But it's you."

I can't tell if the boy in the song is trying to tell the girl he's falling *in* love with her or *out* of love, only that he's sad about whatever it is because it doesn't fit with the person he thinks of himself as being. I wish I could download it on my phone and listen to it ten thousand times.

Maybe the boy in the song is falling *in* love.

Maybe the girl is me.

15

We do peer critiques of our reviews in class on Wednesday. When Ms. Archer stands up to read out the names of the people in each group it occurs to me to really, *really* hope I'm not with Cameron. He did give me condolences for having Hunter as a brother, but he never said anything snarky about Hunter's band, the band about which I've written the most devastating review in the annals of journalism. *His* brother is in the band, too. The band performed one of *his* songs, producing the only line of praise in the entire review, which, now that I imagine Cameron reading it, is over-the-top gushing, and something I'd feel awkward if he read, sitting right there next to me. Of course, he'll be able to read it if the review gets published. But it will feel different then.

If we're in the same critique group, I'm going to have to get a pass for the health room.

We're not.

I get Max Fruh, who's an okay writer but not great; Tyler, who might appreciate the artful nastiness of my review; and Olivia, who would like my review a lot more, I'm sure, if she were the one who had written it.

"So who wants to go first?" I ask after I've led the way in dragging our chairs into a corner of the room as far away from Cameron's group as possible. Olivia isn't the only one who can take a leadership role.

The others shrug.

"Okay, I'll start," I say, pretending I don't care either way.

I pass out copies of the review for them to read. Ms. Archer has us bring four copies to class on peer-critique day.

As they start reading, Ms. Archer pulls up a chair to join us. She likes to circulate from group to group. She never says anything about the piece itself; she just listens to the critique to make sure we're following her guidelines: Start with something positive. Ask questions of the author rather than making assumptions. Don't try to rewrite someone else's piece the way you would have written it. Stay constructive.

I hand Ms. Archer my copy of the review so she can read along.

Please, please, please let her think my review is good enough to be published in the Peaks Post*!*

I hear Tyler chuckle. I wonder which line he just read. Maybe it was "There's bad, there's horribly bad, and then there's Paradox." Or "It's paradoxical how songs by artists as different as John Lennon, Prince, and Coldplay can all end up sounding exactly the same."

Olivia takes the lead again once it's clear everyone has finished reading. This time she's not being bossy: by Ms. Archer's rules, the person sitting to the right of the author facilitates that person's critique.

"So?" Olivia says. "What does anyone like in Autumn's review?"

"It's hysterical," Tyler says. "It's piss-your-pants hilarious. Man, that band must capital S-U-C-K."

"Yeah," Max says. "I liked that part, too." He's the kind of kid who waits to hear what someone else says and then says he agrees with it.

I notice Olivia doesn't say anything *she* likes about it. Instead she says, "I have a question for Autumn. What do you think the reader will *learn* about this band from your review?"

"Um—that they're terrible?" I offer.

"But terrible *how*?" Olivia asks. "Is it their choice of

music that's terrible? Or their playing? What *about* their playing? Are they off-key? Is there something odd about their interpretations? We get that they're loud, but all rock bands are loud. We get a lot of funny insults about the band, but I don't think you really supported them with *examples* and *details*."

I look over at Ms. Archer to see if she's nodding, as Olivia practically quoted her directions to us from last week word for word. But she just sits with her head tilted to one side, the way she does when she's paying close attention.

"Well, I guess I could put more of that part in," I mumble.

What *does* make a band bad? Olivia's question might be fair, but it's hard to answer.

That it has my brother in it isn't going to be enough. *That my brother said even worse things about me* isn't going to be enough either.

"The line about Cameron's song doesn't fit in with the rest," Tyler says.

"Is that the same Cameron as our Cameron?" Max asks. My sudden blush gives the answer away. "I didn't know he wrote songs. Cameron!" Max shouts across the room. "Autumn wrote about you in her review!"

Cameron looks up at the sound of his name.

"She loved your song!" Max shouts.

Well, I did love his song. What's so terrible about that?

"She said"—and now Max is reading aloud from the review, despite Ms. Archer's attempt to shush him—" 'The only redeeming feature of the evening was the haunting ballad by promising songwriter Cameron Miller.' "

Okay. Now I'm cringing almost as much as I did when Hunter read my poem to his friends. I might as well have a big sign hanging around my neck saying AUTUMN GRANGER IS IN LOVE WITH CAMERON MILLER.

But wouldn't Cameron want to know that the only reviewer at the gig thought his song was wonderful? If I had written a song and he had heard it performed and called it a "haunting ballad," I'd be delirious with joy.

Cameron's eyes meet mine but reveal nothing.

To my relief, Tyler focuses our group's discussion back on the substance of what I wrote. "It's an okay line, but I'd like the review better if it was a hundred-percent hating on the band."

"But then it wouldn't be true," I put in, even though another one of Ms. Archer's rules for the groups is that the author isn't supposed to say anything except in reply to a direct question.

"Autumn," Olivia reprimands me.

As if she's never defended herself when a comment is unfair, which she does *all the time.*

"Anything else?" Olivia asks.

Tyler and Max shake their heads.

"Maybe . . ." Olivia begins. "It's just . . . when you're writing a review? Sometimes funny can come out sounding just . . . mean."

So Olivia isn't critiquing my review. She's critiquing *me.*

As always, Olivia looks over at Ms. Archer for her approval.

Maybe Ms. Archer will tell her, *Now, Olivia, remember, we're here to discuss the writing. It's not our job to comment on the character of the writer as a person.*

She doesn't.

She smiles and says, "Thanks for letting me sit in for a while." Not that we had any choice.

Then she heads over to another group.

Did she like my review? Or not?

After all, she's the one who told us that the pen is mightier than the sword. That has to mean that it's okay to use the pen sometimes *as* a sword.

Doesn't it?

16

Olivia's snide comments burn a hole in my heart all morning. But at lunch, when I tell Kylee what Olivia said about my review, she says, "Oh, come *on*. It wouldn't be funny if it was all nicey-nice."

After school Kylee and I get a ride from my mom to the public library. We're supposed to be finding books on the Cherokee Trail of Tears (Kylee) and the Iroquois Confederacy (me) for reports due next week for multicultural history. But first we're looking at the fiction in the YA nook to see if there are any new Creekside Clique books for Kylee or Princess of Paragonia books for me. Even though Kylee is the nicest person at Southern Peaks Middle School, she adores books about mean girls. Even though I'm the daughter of an orthodontist and a homemaker living in suburban sprawl, I devour books about heroic quests and tragic love. Maybe that's not surprising. Readers love to read not only about themselves but also about characters who are as different from them as anyone could be.

Half an hour later we're checking out our books when Kylee says, "Autumn, look."

She points to a poster on the bulletin board by the circulation desk, which publicizes upcoming library events. I scan past flyers for a harpsichord concert, a Russian film festival, and a new lap-sit storytime for babies six to twelve months, and then I see it.

CALLING ALL AUTHORS!

Do you have a novel in progress?

Are you interested in finding out how to get published?

Literary agents Nannerl Keith and Marcy Duhota will share their combined eighteen years of experience: what they are dying to see in a submission, what will make them say "Thanks but no thanks." Come learn how to draw in—or turn off—an agent or editor on your very first page.

The event is on Saturday, November 12 (two and a half weeks away), from one to four in the afternoon. It's free and open to the public. And—this is the part that makes me clutch Kylee's hand—you can bring the first page of your novel for their review. They'll review as many "as time permits." Manuscript pages should be in 12-point Times New Roman type; they should contain no author's names or other identifying information.

"You can bring Tatiana and Ingvar," Kylee says. She knows that's exactly what I'm thinking. "You'll be discovered! They'll read your first page and faint! They'll be like, everyone else go home, we don't want to read your pages now, we just want to read more from this amazing new author!"

"Oh, Kylee, they're not going to say that," I say, even though my fantasy is similar to Kylee's in just about every detail.

"Well, maybe they won't say those exact words," Kylee concedes. "It would be rude to send everybody else away. But I bet they'll say they want to read the rest. Why would they be doing this if they're not trying to find the next *New York Times* bestselling author?"

I study the pictures of the two agents on the flyer. Nannerl Keith has funky glasses and short spiky hair; Marcy Duhota has shoulder-length waves held back with a barrette that makes her look too young to be a literary agent.

Maybe the combined eighteen years of experience is seventeen years for Nannerl and one year for Marcy. But they both look smart and bookish, like people who would stay up all night reading the first volume of a trilogy about a princess (Tatiana) who is trying to break the curse put on her people by a wizard (Ingvar).

What if they *did* want my novel? I know they're agents, not editors, so they wouldn't actually be the ones publishing it; they'd be the ones sending it out to the editors who might want to publish it. I checked out a "how-to-get-published book" once from the library, so that's how I know. But finding an agent is definitely step one. Of course, the book's not even written yet; all I have is seven chapters so far and a tiny bit of the eighth. But if they like it, I could write the rest fast so they could rush it off to some big important editor.

There have been lots of—well, some—mega-popular books that were written and published by kids. S. E. Hinton wrote *The Outsiders* when she was in high school. Christopher Paolini wrote *Eragon* when he was fifteen. Fifteen isn't that much older than twelve. And Christopher Paolini probably didn't have a horrible older brother and a fabulous boy in his journalism class that he needed to impress, or maybe he would have published his book even sooner.

"You're going to go, right?" Kylee presses.

I nod.

It's as if the universe posted this flyer right where I—well, Kylee—had no choice but to see it, just the way the universe put the contest flyer in Ms. Archer's mailbox the very day our personal essays were due in class. It feels so perfect that I found an announcement of a huge knitting opportunity for my best friend and she found an announcement of a huge writing opportunity for me.

Since October 31 falls on a Monday this year, the whole weekend feels like Halloween. On Saturday I spend the morning writing away frantically on Tatiana and Ingvar, now that I have a reason to finish my novel as soon as possible. But then I spend the afternoon working on costumes for Sunday-night trick-or-treating with Kylee, Brianna, and Isabelle. I don't know who decided that Halloween was going to be "observed" on Sunday this year, but apparently it is.

We're over at Isabelle's house. It's a rambling Victorian that I used to think was haunted before I became friends with Isabelle. She's my most scientific, sensible friend, short and a tiny bit squat with big glasses. Brianna is probably the prettiest one of our group, with a halo of golden curls that look fake but are actually real.

Brianna googles "Halloween costumes to make at home" on her phone, since we don't have a lot of money. We end up deciding to be different-colored Crayola crayons, but then we have to get Isabelle's father to drive us to the crafts store to get huge pieces of felt to wrap around ourselves to make the crayon tubes plus the pointed crayon hats, and the felt ends up costing as much money as store-bought costumes would have. Still, we'll look cute trick-or-treating all in a row.

"I hope we see Jack," Isabelle says, once we're back at her house trying to cut the felt without ruining it, given that we have no money to buy more. Jack Turner is the smartest boy in our science class.

I don't expect to see Cameron. I try to imagine him in a costume, and fail.

"Do you think any boys are going to be asking girls to the dance?" Brianna asks.

Kylee and I exchange glances. The dance is on the Friday before Thanksgiving, so still three weeks away. She and I have been to only one dance, the spring dance at the end of sixth grade, which was completely awful. It was just for sixth graders, sort of a "get ready for seventh grade" dance. None of the boys asked any of the girls to dance, or at least no one asked Kylee or me. Candor compels me to report that I did notice Olivia dancing a slow dance with Ryan Metcalf, who is widely regarded as the cutest boy in our grade, though in my view vastly less cute than Cameron. What most of the boys did instead of dancing was get into a popcorn-throwing fight over by the refreshment table, where we were all standing because we had to be doing something so we were scarfing down snacks that weren't even good. Then the popcorn-throwing fight turned into a punch-spilling brawl. Kylee got punch spilled on her best silky white top (the one we spent an hour together choosing), and the stain never came out.

"Maybe," Isabelle says. "I heard that Ryan already asked Olivia."

Why am I not surprised?

In sixth grade, I didn't know Cameron yet because he was off on his family trip around the world. Now that I do know him, the thought of the dance is less hideous than it was before. Though I don't think Cameron is the type to go to a school dance, just as I don't think he's the type to go trick-or-treating. He's not the type to do anything that everybody else is doing.

"What if Henry Dubin invites you?" Brianna asks Kylee.

"I'll say that . . . that . . . I have important knitting I need to do that night," Kylee decides.

"I don't think any boys in our grade are cute enough to go with," Brianna announces, which means she doesn't think Cameron is as cute as I do. Then again, nobody does.

We finish up the costumes in time to order pizza, and on Sunday night we do look pretty great as Scarlet (Brianna), Spring Green (Isabelle), Dandelion (Kylee), and Cerulean (me), all lined up in a row. As I expected, I don't see Cameron out trick-or-treating; in fact, none of us see any boys we know. But we each get a huge, wonderfully disgusting pillowcase full of candy.

On Monday, some teachers and kids come to school in costumes because it's actually Halloween. I'm not wearing a costume, though, and neither is Ms. Archer.

I feel even tenser than usual as I wait for her to hand back our graded reviews. I made some changes before I turned mine in last Friday. Writers have to be able to respond to criticism, even criticism from annoying people like Olivia. I thought up some things to justify the bottom-line conclusion of the band's suckiness: the over-amped sound, the drummer's distracting facial grimaces clearly done on purpose in a mistaken attempt to get attention.

But my heart wasn't in it. Because here's the worst part.

Olivia was right.

My review *was* mean. It was intended to be mean. I went to the gig already knowing the review would be mean before I even heard the band play, and when I heard them play my honest opinion was that I thought they were good. Mean, you might say, was the whole *point*. I know Ms. Archer thought it was mean, too, or at least I thought I saw a hint of approval in her eyes when Olivia said that funny sometimes comes out sounding mean.

She gives me an A–. This is what she writes on it: "Very funny, Autumn! Thanks for your good revisions from the peer-review comments. Perhaps you might be too close to your subject for a completely objective assessment?"

At least she didn't come right out and say I was mean. And her last comment hits home in its absolute rightness. I can't help but love Ms. Archer even more for seeing through me. *Touché, Ms. Archer.*

But I also can't help wishing she had wanted to publish my review in the *Peaks Post*. Did she pick anybody else's instead? She doesn't say anything in class about how we should look forward to reading Olivia's review of Cupcakes Galore! in the next issue, coming out a week from Thursday. (The paper comes out every other week, which is a lot for a middle school newspaper, but most middle schools don't offer a journalism class or have a journalism teacher as amazing as Ms. Archer.)

So maybe she didn't pick Olivia's either.

But she definitely didn't pick mine.

17

After school on Wednesday I'm in Kylee's mother's car with a plastic trash bag filled with a dozen neatly folded dog sweaters. I hope the animal shelter people like her sweaters better than the *New Yorker* people liked my poems or Ms. Archer liked my review. In a million years nobody could ever call Kylee mean. If there were a Nobel Prize for kindness to animals, she'd get it. The sweaters are adorable, with patterns she designed: sweaters with snowflakes, sweaters with dog bones, stars and stripes for the patriotic dog, pine trees with gold stars on top to get dogs into the Christmas spirit. Kylee is kind *and* creative.

"Ms. Archer didn't pick my review to put in the paper," I tell her, though I still haven't made myself tell her about *The New Yorker*. Besides, Kylee will know anyway when the paper comes out next week and my review's not in it. "I guess she agreed with Olivia."

"Oh, pooh," Kylee says, as if nobody could agree with Olivia. "She probably just didn't think enough people were interested in a band that's only played one gig at one coffee shop so far."

That's an excellent point, and one I hadn't thought of when I picked Paradox to write about.

But I notice Kylee looks uncomfortable when she says it, glancing out the window so she won't have to meet my eyes.

Maybe she didn't love my review the way she loved my poems, or at least the way she said she loved them? Maybe she agrees with Olivia more than she wants to say?

Then I notice something even stranger: Kylee's not knitting in the car. It's the first time I haven't seen her knitting since the fateful day I saw the sign.

"You're not knitting."

"I'm knitted out."

"You? Knitted out? Never!"

Come to think of it, she wasn't knitting in journalism today either. I hadn't noticed because Cameron was writing haiku all during class again, rather than doodling. He let me read one of them, and I adored it.

Stones in the river
Hundreds of millions years old
Are used to waiting

I wanted to ask him if this poem had anything to do with his mother saying that his first love was rocks, but there is a limit to how much I can confess to secretly reading over his shoulder.

"I knit so much my fingers were starting to get numb and tingly," Kylee confesses.

"Carpal tunnel syndrome," says her mother from the front seat. "A repetitive stress disorder. The human body wasn't made to knit ten hours a day. We've told Kylee no more knitting for a while."

This is terrible! Poor Kylee!

"What will you *do*?" I ask her.

"I like all kinds of crafts," she says with a cheerful shrug. "My aunt is taking me to a bead show down in Denver this weekend, and she's going to teach me to make these really cool bracelets and necklaces. Forget I told you this: I want you to be surprised when I give you your Christmas present."

Margo, the lady who gave Kylee all the knitting patterns that first day, isn't at the front desk when we arrive at the shelter. Instead there's an unsmiling man who might be in his midtwenties. I sure hope he's good at admiring dog sweaters, after Kylee gave herself carpal tunnel syndrome knitting them nonstop for a month.

"May I help you?" he asks, suspiciously eyeing the bulging trash bag Kylee has carried in, as if it contains a dead animal whose death was Kylee's fault.

"I made some dog sweaters. For the drive?" Kylee unties the drawstring on the bag and begins pulling out the sweaters and laying them on the counter.

"O-M-G!" the man squeals, clasping his hands to his chest.

Never have I seen anybody change so much so fast.

"These are *adorable*! They're *amazing*! I can *so* see this one on Jennifer! And this one on George!"

Kylee flushes with pleasure. Her mother squeezes her shoulder in a proud hug.

Margo appears from a room in the back just as the man is holding up one of the dog sweaters—a patriotic one— and sighing with rapture.

"Oh, my!" Margo's face lights up with pleasure at the sight of Kylee's handiwork. "Jeff, this is the girl I was telling you about. Remember? The one who came back three times to get more yarn?"

I'm so happy for Kylee.

If I had to choose between Ms. Archer loving my review and the animal shelter loving Kylee's sweaters, I might choose the sweaters. I really might.

But I wish the universe had given us both.

We're doing more standard news-and-feature-reporting stuff in journalism for the next few weeks: the five W's (who, what, where, when, why); getting the most important information in the lead; and organizing the piece so that if the editor needs to cut it for reasons of space, he or she can just chop off the end and not lose anything absolutely crucial. I hate the idea of having the ending of any story of mine just lopped off by an editor who happens to be in a lopping mood. I want to be my own lopper.

Our new assignment is a feature piece on someone at our school or in our community who is doing something fascinating. If only I knew something fascinating Cameron was doing and could write about him! Of course, I'd be too shy to ask for an interview, given that I can barely make myself say two sentences to him.

"You're not knitting," I hear Olivia whisper to Kylee in class on Thursday, the day after Kylee delivered her sweaters to the animal shelter. We've all gotten so used to that rhythmic clicking that it feels wrong not to hear it. Maybe even Olivia feels unnerved by the unexpected silence.

We're supposed to be doing a freewrite on the most memorable person we've ever known—I'm doing mine on Cameron while making very sure he can't see what I'm scribbling—but Olivia must be stuck on hers.

I hear Kylee whisper back that she got carpal tunnel syndrome knitting a dozen sweaters for abandoned dogs awaiting adoption at the animal shelter.

"Wow!" Olivia says, sounding nice about Kylee's knitting for the first time.

"Girls," Ms. Archer calls over to them, holding her finger to her lips with a smile.

I think Ms. Archer must miss the sound of Kylee's knitting, too. It's been the sound track for our class all trimester.

"That's so cool!" Olivia whispers to Kylee before she picks up her pen and starts to write. Snarky thought from me: maybe she's decided that the most memorable person she knows is herself.

That evening, Kylee texts me after dinner: **You're not going to believe this.**

I text her back: **What?**

Olivia just called me.

You're kidding.

She wants to write her feature article about me!

About Kylee?

Of course about Kylee.

Who else in our school, who else in any middle school anywhere, knit a dozen stunningly adorable sweaters for stunningly adorable dogs awaiting homes in an animal shelter? And gave herself carpal tunnel syndrome doing it?

This is the article *I* should be writing! Kylee is the memorable person *I* should be writing about! *I'm* Kylee's best friend, not Olivia. Olivia didn't even like Kylee's knitting until Kylee stopped doing it.

Why on earth didn't I think of this before? But I was so distracted by my crush on Cameron that I missed seeing the story of the century—well, at least a terrific piece for the school newspaper and maybe even for the *Broomville Banner*—right in front of my eyes. *This* is the kind of story the Associated Press might pick up, a heart-tugging human interest story with universal appeal.

Could I write it anyway? It's not as if for every story in the world there is only one person who is allowed to write it. Just because Olivia thought of it first doesn't mean I couldn't write it, too, and maybe write it better, because I love Kylee more.

Except: Olivia did think of it first.

And she already talked to Kylee.

I have to face it: on the biggest story in our school this year, she scooped me.

That's great! I text back to Kylee.

And it *is* great for Kylee, it really is, and it's great for Olivia, who found the perfect article idea that was right under my oblivious nose.

The only person it isn't great for is me.

18

I'm once again in the backseat of the car, with Hunter once again at the wheel and Mom once again losing her marbles as she sits next to him. We're making a quick run to the grocery store. I agreed to go because Kylee and Brianna are sleeping over tonight (Isabelle is going to a high school football game with another friend) and I want to pick out exactly which snacks we're having. I could have sent Mom with a list, but sometimes inspiration strikes when I wander the aisles at the store.

So apparently I value spectacular sleepover snacks more than I value my life.

I have to admit Hunter is getting better at driving. There's no lurching now as he steps on the gas. It's almost like being in the car with a normal driver. He stays in his lane just fine with no close calls with parked cars or on-coming traffic.

He drives too fast, though, and doesn't leave enough distance between us and the car ahead of him.

"So what's that rule?" I ask. "The one about how far you're supposed to be behind the other car?"

"Trap," Hunter tells me. He's now said "Shut thy trap" to me so often that he abbreviates it for convenience.

"Hunter, slow down," Mom says. My question had the desired effect. "You're supposed to be two seconds—one one-thousand, two one-thousand—behind that Suburban."

"I am," Hunter says, which is completely false. I'm not sure exactly how the two-second thing is measured, but I'm sure that if the Suburban were to slam on its brakes, we wouldn't have time to stop without rear-ending it.

I guess that wouldn't kill us all.

But it wouldn't be good either.

Hunter gains on the SUV. I can see Mom's neck jerk as she brakes hard. The only problem is she doesn't have a brake.

"Mom!" Hunter barks at her. "You're doing it again! Enough with the imaginary brake!"

"It's a *reflex*," Mom says. "It's an automatic response." She sounds like she's apologizing, which is ridiculous. *He* should be apologizing to *us*.

Hunter turns around to glare at me, as if it's my fault he was driving too close to the SUV in front of us. Even though I said he was getting better at driving, he's not good enough to drive without looking at the road. Few drivers are. Driving-while-giving-your-sister-dirty-looks is just as dangerous as driving-while-texting. Maybe worse.

The car swerves.

Mom shrieks.

She grabs the steering wheel just as we cross the lane into the path of a FedEx delivery truck. I stifle my own yelp of terror.

All I can say is, these snacks had better be worth it. They had better be the best sleepover snacks in the history of the world.

The snacks aren't amazing, but they're good. I've discovered Nutella—this scrumptious chocolate-hazelnut spread—so I bought a jar of it, plus crackers and fruit to spread it on, and vanilla ice cream, because Nutella is the best ice cream topping ever. Also tortilla chips and stuff to make Mom's seven-layer dip (memo to braces-wearing self: don't have any). And cookie dough for these chocolate cookies that have a melted fudgy center.

Kylee and Brianna arrive together after dinner; Brianna had a dinner thing she had to go to with her grandparents. So it's eight-thirty by the time we spread our sleeping bags on the family room floor and open the Nutella jar.

Thank goodness Hunter is sleeping over at Moonbeam's house.

Brianna glances up from her phone, where she is busy texting somebody—Isabelle?—to let her eyes roam around the kitchen and family room. "Where's Hunter?" she asks, as if it would be normal for him to be at home on Friday night to welcome his sister's friends.

"He's out all night, hooray, hooray."

Brianna makes a pouty face.

"No," I tell her. "No. No. No. You are not going to say what I think you're going to say."

"He's cute, that's all," Brianna tells me.

This from the girl who doesn't think a single boy in our grade is cute.

I might just throw up Nutella-covered crackers, which would be a tragedy, because once you've thrown up something, you end up hating the taste of it for a long time afterward. I'll never forgive Brianna if she ruins Nutella for me.

"Try having him for a brother, and then tell me how cute you think he is."

"That thing he does with his eyebrows?" Brianna says. "Where it's like he's teasing you but only because he likes you? And those curls? I've always liked guys with curls. You know, the tousled look. And he's a *drummer*. In a *band*."

I should change the subject, but I can't let those comments go unchallenged. I just can't.

"Well, when he does the stupid eyebrow thing, it's not because he likes *me*, it's because he *hates* me. And his hair would look better if he occasionally washed it. And I wouldn't call him a drummer in a band. I'd call him a 'drummer' in a 'band.'" I make big air quotes with my fingers in case she needs help getting the punctuation marks.

"No one ever thinks their own brother is cute," Brianna says. "Kylee, you're over here all the time. Do *you* think Hunter is cute?"

"Not really," Kylee says loyally. But she's too darned nice to disagree with Brianna outright. "I mean, I can see how *someone* would think he's cute, but he's not my type."

I'm relieved Kylee and I can still be friends. Brianna-as-friend may be on the way out.

"This Nutella is awesome!" Brianna says then, through a big mouthful of Nutella-and-cracker.

I thaw toward her a tiny bit. Even if she has this weird thing for my brother and is obsessed with her stupid phone, at least she loves the same snacks I do.

"Movie time?" I ask. "Something scary or something funny?" I have a row of DVDs lined up on the coffee table next to the snacks.

"Do you know what I heard?" Brianna asks, ignoring my question. Whatever she's going to say is important enough that she actually puts down her phone. "At the student council meeting before school today, we were talking about plans for the dance, and someone suggested having Hunter's band play."

"Who?" I demand.

"Some eighth grader who's friends with *your* big crush, Cameron, though what you see in him I don't know— those bangs falling over his face look soooo lame." Brianna knows I like Cameron, but I'd never, ever tell her about my poems. "Anyway, Cameron's brother is in the band, too, right? And this kid said they're really good."

I can't decide if I'm irritated that Hunter's band might be getting a real gig, or proud of him.

One good thing I can think of is that *if* they play at the dance, Cameron might come in solidarity with them. And *if* he comes, and *if* the band plays his ballad again, and *if* I'm standing right near him, he might ask me to dance. And it might end up being the best night of my life. *If. If. If. If.*

"Scary or funny?" I ask again, trying to get the sleepover back on track. "Who votes for scary?"

Brianna raises her hand.

"Who votes for funny?"

I put up my own hand this time.

"Kylee, you need to vote to break the tie," I tell her.

"Um—both?" she says. "Scary first, then funny, so we're not too scared to sleep."

"Sounds good to me," Brianna says.

So that's what we do, and I eat my way through the Nutella jar, cracker by cracker.

19

Saturday I take a nap to make up for not sleeping at the sleepover, and practice flute, and do a ton of homework for pre-algebra and French. I got the only A in the class on the last test, too, but I didn't tell anyone in my family, to save Hunter the trouble of making more "Whoop-de-doo" comments.

I don't feel like calling anybody to try to do anything tonight, so I lie on my bed and watch a movie on my laptop. I've seen it before: one of my favorite black-and-white movies, *Roman Holiday* with Audrey Hepburn and Gregory Peck.

Audrey Hepburn is a princess who has no freedom to do any fun things ever; she has to do all these stiff, stodgy royal etiquette things instead. But then, on a goodwill tour of European capitals, she runs away for one night, in

Rome, and meets Gregory Peck, who is a reporter for this foreign newspaper. He knows she's a runaway princess, but she doesn't know he knows. They fall in love, but they can't be together because she needs to return to her royal duties. It's more romantic having it end with their not being able to be together than if they had lived happily ever after. The tragic doomedness is what makes it so wonderful.

Hunter likes—well, used to like—black-and-white movies, too. His favorite is *Casablanca*, with Humphrey Bogart and Ingrid Bergman. The first time we watched it together, a couple of years ago, he pointed out all the most famous lines to me: "Round up the usual suspects." "I'm shocked, shocked, to find that gambling is going on here." "We'll always have Paris." "Here's looking at you, kid." It used to be that whenever we came across it on TV, we'd both have to stop whatever we were doing to finish watching it, even though we own it on DVD. But when it was on one night last week, and I plopped down on the couch next to him to watch it, he clicked off the TV and walked away.

So I picked *Roman Holiday* to watch tonight instead. I love *Casablanca* more, but it would make me too sad to watch it now.

It's cold and windy on Sunday after church, so I lie on the couch by the gas fireplace in the family room. I should be working on my novel, because the big day with the two agents at the public library is this coming Saturday, now less than a week away. Instead I'm writing a new batch of poems about Cameron. But I don't write flowery rhyming poems with "thee" and "thou" this time. Hunter's mockery, not to mention the *New Yorker* rejection, has cured me of floweriness. Now I'm striving for the simple style of Cameron's song lyrics.

Maybe my poems could be made into songs, too?

I'll need music to go along with the words. Even though I love playing the flute, I've never tried writing music. Maybe Cameron can collaborate with me: I'd write the lyrics, and he'd come up with the melodies.

Here's the one I wrote that I like best:

> Maybe I care because you don't.
> Maybe I will because you won't.
> And yet I think that if you smiled,
> I'd smile, too.
> And I think that if you left,
> I'd go with you.

I imagine Olivia critiquing my song: "Autumn, what do you think the reader will *learn* from this poem? We get that you like Cameron, but we don't know *why*. What is it *about* Cameron that justifies your feelings for him?"

But Olivia is still the one who knew that Kylee's knitting triumph would make a fabulous article.

And I'm the one who didn't.

Guess who I wrote my feature about? I couldn't think of anyone else, so I wrote about, yes, my father, and how he was named Best Orthodontist in Broomville seven years in a row. What seventh grader writes a "fascinating person" feature about her *dad*? Only a seventh grader who already blew a major chance to write one about her best friend.

The *Peaks Post* is published on Thursday. Olivia's article about Kylee is right there smack in the middle of the front page, complete with a smiling photo of Kylee and pictures of two dogs wearing Kylee's sweaters that Olivia must have gone down to the Broomville Humane Society to take. I don't read it. I can't bear to read it. I don't even let myself collect a copy from the huge piles I see on tables at various points throughout the school hallways. Yet I can't help but see them.

Even as we're standing by our lockers before the first bell, a bunch of girls come up to Kylee to squeal over the article.

"Those sweaters are soooo cute!"

"You should sell them! I want one for my dog for Christmas!"

"Do you think my cat would wear a sweater?"

"Can you make these in people sizes?"

"Can you teach me to knit?"

"We should start a knitting club at Southern Peaks!"

"I never knew so many dogs needed homes!"

Ms. Archer begins journalism class by holding up the hot-off-the-press *Peaks Post* for everyone to see. She does this whenever anyone in the class has an article in it.

"Good morning, intrepid reporters!" she greets us. "I hope you all grabbed your copy of the *Peaks Post* this morning and checked out your classmates' work. We have a terrific feature by our own Olivia Fernandez profiling our own Kylee Willis. Good work, Olivia!"

Olivia flashes Kylee a big grin.

Kylee grins back.

My heart twists.

"And," Ms. Archer continues, "we have an insightful review of Broomville's new knitting store, Knit Wits, by that same Kylee Willis. Nice job, Kylee."

What?

I totally did not see that coming.

How *could* I have seen that coming when my own best friend didn't even tell me that Ms. Archer picked *her* review—*not* Olivia's and *not* mine—for publication?

I wonder if Kylee will turn around and look at me with pleading eyes.

She doesn't.

As the day began, so it continues. Kylee is mobbed in the halls even by kids who don't know her.

"Are you the girl who was in the paper today?"

"Are you the knitting person?"

"That is so cool, what you did."

"Do you need a dog model? I have a dog who would look so great in your sweaters."

I don't say anything to Kylee about the Knit Wits review. If I were a truly good friend, I'd congratulate her on her first publication. But if she were a truly good friend, she would have told me about it ahead of time.

I feel almost as terrible as I did when Hunter showed my poem to the band.

I feel almost as terrible as I did when *The New Yorker* rejected my poems.

Maybe even worse.

After school, my mom is driving us to ballet. Neither of us is talking in the car.

I'm looking hard out of the window—the animal shelter sign says ENROLL FOR PUPPY PREP SCHOOL NOW!—when I feel Kylee's hand reach out for mine.

"I'm sorry," Kylee says.

"For what?" I don't even try to keep the bitterness out of my voice.

"That Ms. Archer picked my review, not yours."

Even as publication-crazed as I am, I know that's not something Kylee should have to feel sorry about. Who knows more about knitting stores than Kylee? Of course, her review would be wonderful. Ms. Archer told us to pick a subject that would draw on our special areas of expertise; she never told us to pick a subject that would allow us to get revenge against somebody who broke our heart. Besides, Kylee's review makes the perfect companion to Olivia's feature.

Kylee totally does not need to apologize to me for getting published first.

"I'm glad she picked your review!" I say. It's even (sort of) true. But then the bitterness creeps back into my voice. "But why didn't you tell me?"

"I just felt so bad. Because I knew you wanted it more. And I wanted it more for you than I wanted it for me."

How can I stay bitter with a friend like this?

"But you're going to get published, too, Autumn," she promises me, as if she has the power to make the promise come true. "You'll get published in a bigger, better place than our school paper. Maybe this is the week you'll hear from *The New Yorker*!"

Now tears blur my vision, not tears of disappointment for my rejection, but disappointment in *me* for not sharing it with Kylee. Who am I to be mad at *her* for keeping a secret?

I shake my head.

She reads the truth from my forced smile and welling eyes.

"Oh, Autumn," she says, squeezing my hand and snuggling up against my shoulder.

Whatever dreams don't come true for me, I have the best friend anybody on earth ever had.

I squeeze her hand back and rest my head against hers, without speaking.

20

We haven't had a family dinner, with all four of us at the table, for days. Dad was away at an orthodontist convention. Hunter's been claiming to be at extra sessions with the band. I had dinner at Kylee's one night because her mom made this special spicy pork-and-noodle dish that I love. But we're all here tonight.

"What's new with you, Autumn?" Dad says. He always starts with me, as if to get some good news before he has to turn to Hunter for the bad news. But today I have no good news. Today I have the total opposite of good news.

"Nothing," I say with false brightness.

"Nothing?" Mom asks.

I thrust out my chin. "Nothing," I repeat. I can be as surly as Hunter when I want to be.

At least there are only two more days until the agents

come to the library and I have a chance to show them chapter one of Tatiana and Ingvar. Plus, there's still the essay contest, though my hopes for it are dimming. Winners are supposed to hear by mid-November; it's already November 10, and I have a feeling I would have heard by now if they read my essay and were enraptured by it.

"Hunter, what's new with you?" Dad asks.

"The band has another gig," Hunter says.

"That's wonderful!" Mom gushes.

"And we're getting paid this time," Hunter adds, unable to keep the pride out of his voice.

For a second I feel as if I'm in some kind of alternative universe, where I'm Goofus and Hunter is Gallant, where I'm the one sitting in sullen silence while he gets to crow about a major accomplishment.

But I'm not going to let him know how jealous I feel.

"To Hunter!" I'm the first one to say, holding up my water glass to start a round of clinks. And once Dad raises his glass, too, I almost do feel happy for Hunter, and happy for me. This is what normal families should be doing, celebrating someone's success with an ice-water toast.

"What *is* the gig?" Mom asks.

"We're playing for the dance at Southern Peaks," he says. I notice he doesn't call it Southern Pukes this time. A school that is paying you to play at their dance can't be all that pukey.

Now I have something else in my life to hope for. Even though my publishing dreams have had some crushing disappointments, the first big *if* of my Cameron-at-the-dance fantasy has come true: Paradox is playing there! Now all I need is for Cameron to come to the dance, and for the band to play his song, and for him to ask me to dance. The first two of these are now pretty likely. So I need to concentrate all my deepest wishing on the final one.

I'm so lost in these thoughts I miss the last couple of things said at the table. Apparently, while I blinked, it all turned not-so-good.

"All I meant," Dad is saying, "is that while it's great that the band is getting gigs, you should consider signing up for some school clubs or activities, too. You're on a roll now! Keep the momentum going!"

"Save the Rhinos?" Hunter asks. "Anime Club? Board Gamers Guild? Like, my life will be totally better if I join the Board Gamers Guild?"

"Okay." Dad forces a smile. "I concede that the Board Gamers Guild is not likely to be a big life changer. But what about the school newspaper, or the debate team, or the knowledge bowl? Or—even if you don't want to do cross-country—surely there is some other sport . . ."

"Oh, Derrick," Mom says. "Let's just celebrate Hunter tonight."

"That's what we're doing," Dad says. "But, Hunter, you're in high school now—"

"Am I? Thanks!" Hunter says. "For a moment there I had forgotten."

Dad's color deepens. Like Mom, I wish he'd get off the why-don't-you-do-a-sport topic. But Hunter's sarcasm is going too far.

Dad continues as if Hunter hadn't interrupted him. "And college admissions committees are going to want to see more on your application than 'drummer in a rock band.' That's a fact. I'm just pointing out a fact."

"Maybe I don't want to go to college," Hunter shoots back.

I wait to see if Dad is going to blow up over this one, but he gives another conciliatory smile, even though it's a condescending smile, too.

"You say that now. But let's see what you're saying two years from now when all your friends are applying to colleges and getting into good places. Your mother and I want you to have choices. We don't want you doing anything now that limits your choices."

"Maybe *my* choices for me are different from *your* choices for me."

"You aren't going to have *any* choices then"—Dad raises his voice—"if you don't start making some different choices *now*. You do realize that report cards come out next week?"

Hunter shrugs.

If there's one thing Dad hates, it's a shrug.

"I hope," Dad says, "that a certain drummer will complete some missing work and turn it in between now and then. I hope that a certain drummer can bring up certain grades to at *least* C's so that he doesn't get grounded. It's hard to play at a dance if you're grounded."

Hunter has already pushed his chair back from the table. He walks upstairs without a backward look at his barely touched make-your-own taco.

Maybe he's gone off for one last-ditch study spurt to get his grades back on track. He could still finish that missing work and turn it in for partial credit. Hunter is smart. He could raise his grades if he tried. He's just never cared enough to try.

"Couldn't we be happy for just one evening?" Mom asks as I hear Hunter's door slam.

"He's not going to get into a decent college with those grades," Dad says wearily. "How happy will we all be then? How happy will *he* be when he gets a dead-end minimum-wage job with no benefits and no future, just a few fifty-dollar gigs now and then? We've tried letting him have his own way, follow his own path, walk away from the cross-country team after one week—one week! Maybe we need to ground him right now, today, this minute, rather than sit around waiting for him to fail next week, or next year, or for the rest of his life. Maybe it's time we imposed some consequences on him, or one of these days the real world is going to be doing that for us."

"Give him one more chance," Mom says. "You've made your point. Let him get that missing work finished on his own. Maybe we haven't trusted him enough."

"Or maybe we've trusted him too much," Dad says.

So Hunter and I are both Goofuses now, and our family has no Gallants at all.

21

When I get to the library for the Calling All Authors event, I see a big sign saying it's in the auditorium. It took longer to bike here than I thought it would, and the auditorium is already packed. Apparently there are a lot of people in the world who want to find out how to get published. Kylee offered to come with me today, for moral support, but I decided this was something I needed to do alone.

Everyone I see is older than I am, and some of them are downright old. One woman has a little oxygen tank she's dragging along behind her; another one hobbles in with a walker. Part of me feels good that such old people still have dreams. But part of me is sad that they've lived so long without having their dreams come true. I want my dreams to come true *now*.

I thought Olivia might be here, but she's nowhere to be seen. I feel a spiteful pleasure in the thought that maybe she didn't even know about it. *Thank you, Kylee!* The *Broomville Banner* picked up Olivia's *Peaks Post* feature on Kylee, so now Olivia has been published not only in our school paper but also in a real grown-up paper that thousands and thousands of people read each day.

There's a box by the entrance with a handmade sign that says, "First pages." Now that the moment has come, I hate the thought of surrendering my precious page to the box with all the others. This must be why my mother cried as she was videoing me walking into school on the first day of kindergarten. Should I put my page on top? I decide to tuck it into the middle of the pile. The pile is getting thick, with maybe thirty or forty first pages in it. Maybe time won't permit the agents to get to mine. Wouldn't it be heartbreaking to be the one they were just about to read before time ran out? I retrieve mine from the middle of the pile and put it on the top again. But it would be unfair to read them in that order, with the latest arrivals read first. They'd probably shuffle the pile, right? I put my page back in the middle again.

The program starts ten minutes late, which is agonizing. But finally the library lady introduces Nannerl and

Marcy, who both look a lot older than their pictures. They start out by telling us how hard it is to get published. Last year Nannerl got forty-three hundred submissions from authors seeking representation; she accepted three as her clients. Marcy got forty-six hundred; she accepted one.

I *should* have brought Kylee with me. Instead I have to tell myself what she'd be whispering if she were there beside me: *Somebody has to be the one. Why not you?*

They tell us they're going to be "brutally honest." That's fine. I can take brutally honest. Lately I've had plenty of practice.

The way this is going to work is that the library lady will read aloud the first pages. As she reads, the agent ladies will tell her to stop at the point they would have stopped reading if this had been a real submission at their real office in real life.

"Okay?" Marcy asks, as if they'd change the procedure if someone said no.

I feel the palms of my hands getting damp and clammy.

This is scarier than I thought it would be.

They interrupt the first reading after *two sentences*. It's a picture book for young kids about Sammy Squirrel and Charlie Chipmunk.

"No anthropomorphized animals," Marcy says. I figure

out that this means: no animal characters that look and act like humans.

"No alliterative names," Nannerl says.

I'm grateful Tatiana and Ingvar are humans. Well, Ingvar is a wizard, but I think wizards are still technically human. I'm grateful their first and last names don't start with the same letter.

The second story is about a girl who is staying at her uncle's ruined mansion in the Yorkshire moors. In the first sentence she's about to open the door to a forbidden attic. I think it's terrific: lots of deliciously creepy atmosphere, with something exciting happening right away to catch the reader's attention. But Nannerl and Marcy cut off reading after what sounds like the first paragraph. It turns out both of them hate any story that has a forbidden attic. Apparently forbidden attics are used too often. Who knew?

Thank goodness Tatiana and Ingvar's story has no forbidden attic in it anywhere.

Another story opens with a wonderful first line: "If only I had never glanced out the window on that fateful Tuesday, everything would have been different."

But that's the very line that dooms it in Marcy and Nannerl's opinion. They said the line was a cliché.

Well, some things become clichés because they *work*. That line worked for me. I wanted to know: *What* did the narrator see through that open window? *How* did it change everything?

As submission after submission gets rejected, I almost start to hope time won't permit them to get to mine. Except I still can't help hoping they will. So far, mine doesn't have a single one of the things they hate.

They come to one they like. It's a funny story about a boy on a ranch that has a weird name: the No Luck Ranch. The boy is trying to win a llama-raising contest. Marcy praises the "voice." Marcy praises the "humor." I had thought they might have some rule against weirdly named ranches. But both of them say this one makes them want to read on.

The library lady picks up the next one and begins to read.

" 'Tatiana Rostoff tried to scream.' "

I try to listen objectively, as if I hadn't written it. Reacting with complete objectivity, I like it so far, I do, I do! I like her name. Why does she want to scream? Why is she failing to scream? Because "tried to" suggests unsuccessful activity. Those five simple direct words have intrigued me. I want to read on. I want to publish the book!

" 'No sound escaped her. Smothered beneath the weight

of the silken coverlet pressed against her face, she heard a man's voice, all the more menacing because he spoke in a muffled whisper, "Tell the secret or you will die!"'"

I love the silken coverlet. It hints at wealth and royal status. *Smothered* is a strong verb. The contrast between the violent message and the whispered tone catches my attention. *What* secret? Why does he want to know it so badly?

"'Tatiana awoke from her dream to find herself cowering beneath her velvet bed curtains as pale sunlight filtered through the lead-paned windows of the castle.'"

Love the pale sunlight! Love the lead-paned windows!

"Stop," Nannerl says.

"Stop," Marcy agrees.

Stop?

"Dream," they say together.

"The worst of all openings is beginning with a dream," says Marcy.

"Other people's dreams are inherently uninteresting," says Nannerl. "If you want to bore someone at a party, start telling them your dreams."

But one of my favorite books ever, *Rebecca* by Daphne du Maurier, begins with one of the best lines ever: "Last night I dreamt I went to Manderley again." It's true Daphne du Maurier doesn't trick the reader into thinking the opening dream sequence is really happening, but she still starts with a dream. Would these two agents reject *Rebecca*, too?

The library lady is already starting to read the next submission. Guess what? It starts with a dream. And so do the two submissions after that! The audience actually starts laughing on the fourth one when the library lady reads the line "Jacob awoke, heart pounding, from his dream."

Would I feel even worse if I were this fourth dream-beginning author? Or was it worse to be me, sitting there like a happy idiot, still hoping they'd praise my voice, my dramatic timing, my ability to create an instant rapport with the reader?

I'm glad I didn't bring Kylee with me. I feel hurt not only on my behalf but on hers, too, as if *she* had just been mocked for being dumb enough to think my writing was good, dumb enough to *believe* in me.

I should leave. Once two agents with a combined eighteen years of experience destroy your dream, why stay? But I don't want to call attention to my flaming cheeks and trembling lips, signaling to everyone around me that I was one of the capital-*C* Clueless authors who thought it was a brilliant idea to start a story with a dream.

Just then Marcy and Nannerl finish rejecting the next submission, and the library lady says, "Let's take a ten-minute break—we have some cookies and lemonade set up for you in the lobby—and we'll reconvene at two-thirty."

I do *not* plan to reconvene.

I plan to go home and put Tatiana and Ingvar into the shredder my mother keeps for bank statements and tax stuff. No, I'll burn them in the fireplace. Ours has a gas-insert thing, but it still burns with a real flame.

And I do *not* want any cookies and lemonade.

I'm in the lobby, shoving my arms into my jacket sleeves and strapping on my bike helmet when Nannerl, the agent with the glasses and spiky hair, the one who said, "If you want to bore someone at a party, start telling them your dreams," comes up to me.

"Are you all right?" she asks.

I feel as if she just ran over my newborn kitten with a twenty-ton trash truck, scraped the kitten's last bits of blood-spattered fur off her huge studded tires, and then asked me, "Is everything okay?"

But her voice is kind, and I'm already three-quarters of the way to blubbering, so now I'm all the way there, and tears are spilling out of my eyes and running down my face.

"Which one was yours?" she asks gently.

"The first dream one."

"Oh." It's clear she's not quite sure what to say now. "I'm sorry . . . I have to say, Marcy and I didn't expect to be critiquing anybody your age. This program was targeted to serious writers who are ready to seek publication."

But that *is* me! I'm a serious writer! I'm seeking publication harder than anyone!

Maybe now she'll say she liked the lead-paned windows. Or that mine was by far the best of the four dream pieces. Or that if I revised the opening to delete the dream, she'd want to read more.

She doesn't.

"Don't give up," she says. "Promise me you won't give up."

But *The New Yorker* rejected my poems, and Olivia scooped the Kylee article, and Ms. Archer picked Kylee's review over mine. Now two agents with a combined eighteen years of experience made fun of my novel in front of a packed auditorium. I haven't proved a thing to Hunter. I certainly haven't made Cameron fall in love with the wonderfulness of my words.

Without a syllable, I turn away from her and head outside, where it's raining now, and I pedal home.

22

November 15 falls on a Tuesday. If the essay contest people are going to notify winners by "mid-November," this is as "mid" as "mid" can be. I check my email all day long—before classes, after classes, surreptitiously under my desk during classes: nothing. Maybe they'll tell us by snail mail, not email? But when I check the mail first thing when I get home after school: nothing. The *New Yorker* editor emailed me on a Saturday, so maybe the contest judges work odd hours, too. But when I go to bed at ten, I've still heard nothing. I reach for my phone to check my email first thing when I wake up Wednesday morning, and keep checking it all day Wednesday. Ditto for Thursday.

Nothing.

It's starting to look as if I have a clean sweep of failure at everything.

After ballet on Thursday I go to Kylee's house for dinner, and we make necklaces together with the beautiful handcrafted glass beads she got at the bead show in Denver. She keeps saying that the agents were wrong and my novel is wonderful, but it's hard to let myself believe her. Well, if I'm no longer going to be a writer, maybe I can be a necklace maker. I don't think there's as much rejection in necklace making. There isn't any equivalent to a *New Yorker* necklace magazine. As far as I know, there aren't any brutally honest necklace agents.

Friday is the last day before our weeklong Thanksgiving break. It's also the day of the middle school dance, when Cameron might or might not be there, and the band might or might not play his song, and he might or might not ask me to dance. It's a day fraught with fraughtness.

We get our report cards eighth period, which for me is science with Mr. Cupertino. Isabelle is the only one of my friends who is in that class with me. Even though parents can check grades on Infinite Campus, we get a paper printout of them in an envelope for us to take home for our parents to sign, in case there are some parents who aren't as obsessed with Infinite Campus as my parents are. Plus, some teachers take forever to update the website, which drives parents like mine absolutely foaming-at-the-mouth crazy, but all teachers *have* to turn in all the grades for report card day. And report card day is when our grades become real and final.

When Mr. Cupertino hands out the envelopes, I channel Cameron and don't open mine. I put it in my science binder without even peeking.

"How'd you do?" Isabelle asks as we head to our lockers after the dismissal bell.

I shrug. "I don't know. I haven't looked yet."

She stares.

I smile.

Maybe this is why Cameron is the way he is. It's lovely to feel so strong and pure, indifferent to what everyone else is worried about. Like I'm standing outside in a driving rain and everyone else is huddled under their umbrellas moaning about how wet their feet are getting, and not a drop of rain is falling on me. Or maybe it *is* falling, and I just turn my face up to the sky and say, *Oh. Water.*

Of course, the minute no one is looking, I stand by my open locker, slip the envelope out of the binder, and open it.

All A's except for a B in pre-algebra.

Kylee appears next to me, ready to walk home together.

"What are we doing this weekend?" she asks. I love that she doesn't say anything about her report card or ask anything about mine. In her own way, Kylee is as cool as Cameron.

"Sleep?" I suggest. "You could knit?" Kylee's parents have allowed her to knit again, with a one-hour-a-day limit.

In the past I would have said, *Write*, but I still feel too terrible from Calling All Authors, which should have been titled Destroying All Authors. I didn't end up actually burning my novel—I couldn't do it—but I don't want to write anything ever again, except what I have to write for journalism class. As it turns out, I'm not someone who thrives on massive rejection and gets stronger and tougher from brutally honest criticism. I'm someone who thrives on encouragement and praise. Of which lately I've been getting precisely none.

I push these thoughts from my mind. "And tonight we have—"

"The dance," Kylee says. "Are we definitely going? Because last time—"

"This dance will be different," I promise. "The sixth-grade one was just supposed to be an experiment to see how we'd do."

Kylee laughs at the obviousness of the experiment's

results. We're outside now, in the mob of kids searching for their parents in the long line of cars idling in front of the school. I'm glad Kylee and I live close enough that we can walk.

"There won't be any sixth graders at this one," I tell her. "Just seventh and eighth graders. No popcorn war. No punch disaster. This will be a dance where people actually dance."

It might even be a dance where Cameron dances with me.

"Okay," Kylee says. "We'll go. But we're not standing by the refreshment table. And if Henry Dubin asks me to dance, I'm just going to say . . . What am I going to say?"

"You'll say that you're sorry, but you were just about to go to the bathroom."

"What if I get back from the bathroom and he asks me a second time?"

"You'll say that you have to go to the bathroom again. It must have been something you ate."

"So you'll be out there dancing with Cameron"—I haven't told her my fantasy, but she figured it out on her own—"while I'm spending the night in the bathroom pretending to have diarrhea?"

"Yes," I say. "That's the plan."

People walk past us, still talking about their report cards.

"I had an eighty-nine, and I can't believe she didn't round it up to an A . . ."

"Mr. Pearson only likes you if you laugh at his jokes, and, believe me, they are the dumbest jokes you've ever heard . . ."

"My dad is going to kill me . . ."

We're crossing the bridge on the creek a block away from the school. Yes, our school was built on a flood plain. Any time we get a long rain kids start hoping the school will be flooded and classes will be canceled. It's never happened yet, but it might someday.

"Look," Kylee says, stopping suddenly, halfway across the bridge. "Is that Cameron?"

There's a kid, facing away from us, standing on a flat rock in the middle of the creek.

It *is* Cameron.

"What's he doing?" Kylee asks.

He's stacking rocks, one on top of the other, placing each one carefully on the one below so they're perfectly balanced. He's not arranging them in order of size, little ones on top of big ones. That would be too boring. That would be too easy.

My mother says the first thing I ever loved was rocks.

The wind has come up, but Cameron isn't wearing a jacket. His tennis shoes must be soaked with the creek water rippling against them.

Now I see there are several rock towers in the creek, each one constructed from five or six rocks, each one different. Did Cameron make them all? He wouldn't have had time to make them all today; the bell rang just ten minutes ago. Does he make a new one every day? Or is there a community of rock artists, who might even be strangers to each other, coming in solitude to make their own rock sculptures and then go on their way?

"What if someone comes and knocks them down?" Kylee asks in a low voice. "Or the wind topples them over? They're not held together with glue or anything."

I don't answer. I'm too busy watching Cameron, who clearly doesn't care about permanence or publication, who wouldn't be upset by what two literary agents said about him if he even bothered to listen.

The rock formations are beautiful, but it's even more beautiful to watch him in the process of creating, like watching a ballet with only one lone dancer on the stage, and no audience.

Except for us.

As Cameron places the final rock on top, he stands back to survey his work. That's when he looks up and sees us.

It would be wrong, it would feel crass, to shout a big friendly greeting. *Hey, Cameron!*

Kylee seems to know this, too. She's intuitive that way, plus she's not a shouty person in the first place.

He raises one hand to us in a silent gesture.

We give small waves in return.

"Let's go," I whisper.

We keep on walking.

"That was cool," Kylee says a block later. "Sort of . . . magical."

"Yeah," I say. "It was."

23

I wonder sometimes what other families are like. I've been to Kylee's house, of course, and to Brianna's and Isabelle's and other friends' houses over the years. But you never get to see what those families are like when you aren't there.

Here's what I'm wondering about today: In other families, do people *know* so much about each other? Like, do most kids bring home their report cards and everyone sits around sharing their grades in a little report card ceremony? Or do most parents talk to each kid in private, so Billy doesn't know Sally's grades, and Sally doesn't know Billy's? Are there families that believe in *privacy*?

My family doesn't. Or even if we *believe* in privacy, somehow it turns out nobody ever has any.

Hunter isn't home when I get there, and Dad is at work,

so I leave my report card on the kitchen table for Mom to see.

"Very nice, sweetie," she says, after studying it for a minute, as if it takes a full minute to analyze a line of A's with one B. I bet she waited to comment because part of her wants to say, *What happened in math?* But she knows it would be unfair to make a stink about my one B when Hunter will be lucky to have a single B.

My mother sets my report card back on the table and laces her fingers together in a tight weave. "I just hope . . ." she says.

She doesn't need to conclude the sentence because, even after how awful Hunter has been to me, I'm still hoping the exact same thing. Maybe Dad didn't really mean the threat about grounding him if his grades weren't acceptable. Our parents have never been ones for threats, but Brianna's parents make threats all the time that they never follow through on, like "If you can't stop texting while I'm talking to you, I'm going to cancel the text feature on your phone." I've heard that one at least three times, and I don't even go over to her house very often.

"He just wants what's best for Hunter, you know," Mom tells me then. "What's best for both of you. We're proud of *your* grades, of course, but middle school grades . . . they

181

don't follow you through life the same way that high school grades do. Hunter's grades *count*. And we wouldn't be so hard on him if we didn't know he's bright enough to do better if we could just get him to focus."

It feels strange to be talking with my mother about my brother as if we're two adults. But I know she knows I'm worried, too.

"Maybe it will all be okay," I say. But then I realize: she already knows what his grades are. The Infinite Campus website would be totally updated now; the report card is printed right off it. What she hopes is that Dad won't freak out too much about them.

"This band," she says, still flexing her clenched fingers. "I'm not sure if it's the source of the problem, or if it's a positive thing. I generally think people should follow their dreams, though I know your father worries about this particular dream. And the other boys in the band . . . Don't tell Hunter, but I talked to their parents, and they all seem to be doing fine in school right now, even Moonbeam."

The way she says "even Moonbeam" cracks me up. There's so much suggested by that one word: "even."

She smiles. "That name! Oh, well, one thing about names is you can change them whenever you want and then change them back again. I was Suzy-with-a-y in third grade, and then Suzie-with-an-i-e in sixth grade, and then

Suze in high school, and now I'm Suzanne. And if I went through a New Age phase and decided to call myself Starshine, I could be Suzanne again any time I wanted. It's easy to change a name."

She opens her hand to smooth my report card sheet.

"Unlike a grade."

Dad gets home before Hunter does. I'm in the kitchen, helping Mom dice carrots and celery for another healthy Asian stir-fry. I can tell from the grim set to his jaw that he checked Infinite Campus and already knows what Hunter's final grades for the trimester turned out to be even without a paper printout.

"Maybe," Mom says, once Dad has shrugged off his jacket and hung it on the hook by the back door, "we can just let him play for Autumn's dance? He's worked so hard for it. And we don't have to call it 'being grounded.' We can just say we're limiting outside activities for a while so he can focus better on his schoolwork."

"Kylee's parents limited knitting for a while," I pipe up. "Because she was getting carpal tunnel syndrome from making all those dog sweaters. But they let her finish making the sweaters first. And now they're letting her start knitting again."

My parents whirl around to look at me. I think for a

moment they forgot I was there. One of the things you learn as a writer is how to make yourself invisible so that people will say all kinds of things in front of you. I turned myself invisible once at church. I was sitting in a corner of the church kitchen rolling up silverware in napkins for a church dinner, and I heard the lower elementary Sunday school teacher telling the middle school Sunday school teacher about her marital problems, which would be extremely useful if I were still a writer and planning to write a grown-up novel.

"Oh, honey," Dad says. "Let your mom and me do the worrying here."

"Fine," I say cheerfully. Someone in this family has to be cheerful. "How about I go read for a while, and you can call me when dinner is ready."

Dad's face softens. "Believe me, Autumn, the hardest part of parenting is making decisions that your kids don't like now but will thank you for later." He gives me a quick kiss on the cheek before I head upstairs.

It's half an hour later when I hear the front door open and shut, then voices in the kitchen, and then Hunter's angry shout.

"This is so stupid!" Hunter yells. "You're starting the grounding *now*? How's *that* supposed to help my grades? I don't have any homework for a whole freaking week! The trimester's over! What am I supposed to do, sit around staring at you and Mom and Autumn?"

I hear Dad: "You can't say we didn't tell you, as clear as clear can be, what would happen if you didn't get that missing work completed in time. If we don't give you some little consequences now, then the world is going to give you some big consequences later."

It's the same thing he told Mom after the dinner-table fight the other night, so either he really believes it or he's trying very hard to talk himself into believing it.

I don't hear the next thing Hunter says or what Dad says after that. I can't tell if Mom is part of the conversation or not.

Then: "I have a *gig*! I can't miss my *gig*! It's a *commitment. You're* the one who always tells us we have to honor our *commitments*!"

Feet pounding on the stairs.

Door slamming.

I hear something that, if I didn't know Hunter never cries, might sound an awful lot like crying.

Hunter doesn't come down for dinner.

"He'll come out sooner or later," Dad says, as if he's hoping desperately that this is true. He glances across the table at Mom, but she looks away. I know she's hoping against hope that he'll relent on the grounding, but he's not going to turn back. It's clear he thinks they should have grounded Hunter weeks ago for his slipping grades.

Dad sighs then. "If he wants to turn 'being grounded' into 'solitary confinement,' I guess that's his choice."

"No, it isn't," Mom says. "No child of mine is going to go hungry in this house. Grounded or not grounded, he's a growing boy. He needs to eat. Autumn, honey, if I fix a tray, will you take it up to him?"

Why does she think he'll take a tray from me any more than from her?

On the tray Mom puts a plate of stir-fry and brown rice, a glass of milk, and a cut-up apple, plus a napkin and silverware. I bet if she had a single rose to put in a bud vase, she'd add that, too.

After I carry the tray upstairs comes the scary part.

I tap on Hunter's door. Loud enough that he'll hear—unless he has his earbuds in and his music turned up high—but still more of a timid plea on my part.

No answer.

"Hunter? It's me. Autumn."

No answer.

I push the door open a crack. Hunter is lying on his bed, glaring at me.

"Mom sent me with this." I set the tray down on the floor. There's no other available surface to put it on, and even the floor is covered with so many dirty clothes I have to push a pair of Hunter's jeans out of the way with my foot. Then I continue my spurt of tidying by shoving Hunter's hoodie and a crumpled, smelly T-shirt out of the way, and I sit down on the floor next to the tray, clasping my legs to my chest in my usual scrunched-up little ball.

"Mom feels bad," I say.

Hunter makes no response.

"Dad feels bad, too."

"Yeah, right."

At least he's talking now.

I swallow hard. "I feel bad."

If I thought this might turn into a moment of brother-sister closeness, I was wrong.

"Shut up," Hunter says. No genteel "Shut thy trap" this time. Actually, he says, "Shut the something up," using a word that is so much worse than mere "Shut up" that my mom hasn't even felt the need to make a rule against it.

"Don't you ever get sick of yourself?" he sneers. "Sick of being Miss Perfect all the time? Perfect grades? 'Oh, I got the only A in the class on the French exam.' Perfect flute solos? Perfect pirouettes in your perfect ballets?"

I blink back tears.

"I'm not Miss Perfect."

I'm not anywhere near perfect. *The New Yorker* didn't think my poems were perfect. Ms. Archer didn't think my review was perfect. The two agents didn't think my novel was perfect. The essay contest judges didn't think my essay was perfect.

Right this minute I don't even want to be perfect. I just want to have my big brother back again.

I try again over the lump in my throat. "Hunter, why are you so mean to me all the time?"

What I want to say is, *I still love you, Hunter. Why don't you still love me?*

"Give it up, Autumn," Hunter says. "Just get up, walk away, and don't come back."

How could I have thought, one second ago, that I loved him, this brother who is looking at me with icy eyes and sneering mouth? What did I ever do to him that he treats me like his worst enemy, mocking me and my poems, and refusing to let me into his life anymore in even the teensiest, most minimally friendly way? I'm not the reason he got grounded.

"I hate you, Hunter." My voice is trembling. "I'm glad you can't play at our dance, and I hope you fail out of school, and Mom and Dad kick you out, and you end up hungry and homeless with no one to bring you any tray of food again, ever."

I follow Hunter's nasty instructions and get up off the floor, ready to walk out on him and never return. But before I do, I say the one thing that never in a million years would I have dreamed I could say.

"I wish you were dead."

24

I'm not really in the mood for going to the dance now, but Kylee and I go anyway.

The dance has a theme: Beach Party. The wearing of tropical-inspired outfits has been encouraged, but Kylee and I are both just wearing short black dresses (but not the kind of short black dresses that would make our dads send us back upstairs to change). When Kylee and I show our IDs and get our hands stamped at the gym door, I can see that only half a dozen boys are wearing Hawaiian shirts and the rest are in ordinary T-shirts and jeans. The only evidence I can see of the dance theme in the girls' attire is that a few girls have flowers in their hair. One of them (the one with the longest, thickest, most flower-worthy hair) is Olivia, of course. The rumor that Ryan Metcalf asked her to the dance turns out to be true.

To further the beach theme, surfboards are propped up against the gym walls next to travel agency posters advertising vacations in Aruba and Tahiti. Beach towels are spread out over part of the floor, with a few seashells scattered here and there.

Even as I take in the decorations and the outfits, the things I really care about are (1) whether Cameron is there and (2) whether Paradox is playing without their drummer.

The answer to the first question is: I don't see him. But that doesn't mean anything. It's fairly dark in the gym, and there are a lot of seventh and eighth graders crowded around the still completely empty dance floor.

The answer to the second question is: Some band is playing right now and it's definitely Paradox. I would recognize David Miller's throaty voice anywhere. I don't hear a drum.

It's hard to be heard over the sound of the music, but Kylee follows me when I lead the way to the corner of the gym near where the band has set up.

I see David, lead guitar and vocals; Timber, backup guitar and vocals; Moonbeam on bass; and an empty spot where Hunter's drums should be. Paradox must not have found a sub on such short notice. Or—the thought occurs to me—maybe Hunter didn't tell them he was grounded?

Maybe, up until the last possible minute, he thought Dad might relent and let him play? I think Mom thought that might happen, too.

Despite all those hateful things I told Hunter two hours ago, I suddenly feel so terrible for my brother I can hardly stand it. It's too awful for him to finally have a real paid gig at a real dance—with at least a hundred people there—and not be able to sit on his drummer's throne, in his glory. If he didn't tell the rest of the band, if he just didn't show, maybe they'll kick him out, and he won't even be a band member anymore. After weeks of nonstop rejection, I know better than anyone how it feels when a dream dies. I couldn't wish that on anyone, not even on Hunter.

Kylee and I find Brianna by the refreshment table with a couple of other girls we know. It already looks as if this dance may repeat the sixth-grade dance, with Kylee and me huddled by the refreshment table all night, despite my promises to her that it would be different this time.

The food looks great, though. Some of the middle school supermoms went all out on killer snacks. There's a huge fruit display spilling from hollowed-out pineapples, punch with kiwi slices floating on top, a mountain of cheese cubes surrounded by a sea of crackers (the cheese made tropical by a few little paper umbrellas stuck here and there for effect), and a coconut-frosted cake.

192

"Nobody's dancing," I mouth to Brianna.

"It's too early," Brianna mouths back.

Maybe this means there is still time for Cameron to appear. But a quarter of an hour later, I still don't see him. I've eaten two pieces of cake, downed three paper cups of punch, and added a paper umbrella to my hair. No one has asked either Kylee or me to dance, though Brianna is now chatting with a boy from our multicultural history class named Todd, and Jack from science class, who has glasses as big as Isabelle's, is looking her way. Except for the lack of a popcorn-throwing, punch-tossing melee, this definitely feels like the sixth-grade dance all over again.

Mr. Cupertino, my science teacher, who is also the student council adviser, comes over to the microphone set up near the band. He's decked out in a loud-patterned red, orange, and blue Hawaiian shirt, khaki shorts, and flip-flops, with a flower lei hung around his neck. I've noticed that middle school teachers take school spirit stuff more seriously than the students do. He gives a signal to the band to stop playing.

"Good evening, Southern Peaks seventh and eighth graders!" he booms into the mike. "Who's ready for a beach party?"

The question suggests he realizes that the beach party proper has yet to begin.

The crowd gives a good-natured whoop in reply, mainly to humor him. Mr. Cupertino is a good teacher, fair and encouraging, and he did make a special effort to dress up as a beach-party host. I forgot to say that he also covered his nose with that thick white sunblock paste lifeguards wear. The applause of the dance attendees, I think, is chiefly for Mr. Cupertino's nose.

"The band is going to take a short break to rearrange a few things. Before they do, let's give a big hand for Paradox!"

The applause is louder this time. A lot of kids think it's cool to have a real band instead of a DJ. It makes it seem more like a real dance. Of course, at a real dance you'd expect more people to be dancing. And you'd expect a real band to have a drummer.

"And, beach partiers," Mr. Cupertino continues, "when the band returns, let's show them how fast we can fill up a dance floor, shall we?" He must be reading my mind. "To get the beach ball rolling, I'm going to announce boys-ask-girls dances and girls-ask-boys ones, at least for the next few numbers. So go grab some cake and punch"— he's clearly not talking to me and Kylee, who so far have done nothing tonight *but* grab cake and punch—"and get ready to warm up those dancing feet!"

With the band on break, we can actually talk.

"Do you see Cameron anywhere?" I ask Kylee.

"No," she says. "Do you see Henry Dubin?"

"No," I say.

Cameron is too cool to come. Henry isn't cool enough. Kylee and I are smack-dab in the middle zone of coolness, which right now is an awkward place to be.

"What's happening with the band?" Kylee asks.

I whirl around toward Paradox to see what she's talking about, when who should I see coming through the gym door that leads out to the parking lot but Cameron.

He's carrying a large drum in a drum case.

Behind him, carrying two smaller drums, is Hunter.

25

I feel so relieved that Dad relented—Hunter's really only missed about a half hour of the dance so far, the half hour when nobody was even dancing yet—that I almost follow Cameron and Hunter back outside to help drag in the rest of the drums. Maybe there would be some romantic moment when I'd go to pick up an especially heavy one and Cameron would say, *Let me do it*. Maybe one drum would be too heavy for either one of us to carry alone, so the two of us would hoist it together, and our fingers might touch accidentally on purpose.

Instead I just stay with Kylee and eat another piece of coconut cake. I know this makes it sound like I have food issues, when I really don't. Except, apparently, at dances. Especially dances where my grounded brother has miraculously been ungrounded, and the boy I'm in love with has finally shown up. I try to catch Hunter's eye, but he's busy tinkering with the drums. For a moment I think maybe he sees me, but if he does, he looks away so fast I wonder if he somehow wants me not to know he's there, as if I could possibly miss seeing him.

I make it a point not to look at the band anymore. In fact, I make it a point to leave the gym altogether and go to the restroom to comb my hair in the mirror very, very slowly. And remove three pieces of pineapple from the braces on my front teeth.

By the time I get back, the band is playing a fast, throbbing eighties song, with Hunter's drums adding a pounding beat. This is really a dance now. I can see Kylee dancing, not with Henry Dubin, but with Tyler from journalism, who said my review of the band was hilarious.

I approve.

I don't see Cameron among the dancers, for which I'm glad. I don't want him dancing with anyone but me. But then I worry I don't see him anywhere. *Please, please, please don't make it that he came to help the band set up and left already!*

I return to my post by the coconut cake, where I do *not* have a fourth slice, because that would cross the line from understandable stress eating to flat-out-disgusting piggery, plus I do not want any other food morsels stuck in my braces. I take a paper cup half full of punch and pretend to sip from it, to have something to do with my hands.

As I take another fake sip, Cameron appears beside me. I didn't see him approaching. His ability to materialize out of nowhere only adds to his mystique and awesomeness.

I wait for him to speak first.

"Hey," he says.

"Hey," I say in reply.

We both stand watching the dancers. Now I'm glad the music is so loud. It's pleasant to have a ready-made excuse not to try to talk.

Too soon, the song ends. Most of the dancers leap apart, as if terrified by the possibility that they might be stuck together twice in a row. Not Kylee and Tyler, though. He says something to her, and Kylee laughs. Cameron is still standing next to me, gazing out at the dance floor with a vacant kind of stare. Maybe he's writing a haiku in his head. Maybe he's thinking of another rock formation he wants to create.

Mr. Cupertino comes to the mike again.

"Gentlemen, you've had your turn. Ladies, go to it!"

If only Mr. Cupertino had announced the girls' choice first, while I was in the bathroom! It would have been perfect to have a boys' choice happen now, with Cameron standing two feet away from me.

Should I ask him to dance?

I could.

No, I couldn't.

The band starts to play, and it's a *slow dance*. At first I don't recognize the song—after all, I only did hear it once before in my life—but then Cameron's brother begins to sing the first lines: " 'I tell myself that I don't care . . . But I do. I tell myself that it's just me. But it's you.' "

Cameron's song. My song. Our song.

My fantasy is coming true in every single detail. Except for one. *Oh, Mr. Cupertino, why couldn't you have had this be the boys' choice? Why? Why? Why?*

Then—OMG—yes, yes, yes, YES—Cameron looks over at me and jerks his head toward the dance floor. The head jerk has to mean that he's asking me to dance. I must have some kind of psychic power I never realized, to will into being whatever I want most in the world.

Cameron doesn't even care that this is a girls' choice. Of course he doesn't care. He's *Cameron*. He doesn't follow rules, especially trivial rules about who should be doing the inviting for the next dance.

Miraculously, I have the presence of mind to reach

behind me and drop my empty punch cup in the overflowing trash can.

Cameron leads the way to the dance floor.

I tell myself that it's just me. But it's you . . .

I wait for him to put his arms around me. Not the boy's-left-hand-around-the-girl's-waist and the girl's-right-hand-on-the-boy's-left-shoulder thing we learned in a doomed ballroom dancing unit in elementary school P.E. At real dances—and this dance is feeling realer by the minute—the boy puts both of his hands around her waist, holding her close to him, and she puts both of her arms around his shoulders. That's what all the couples around us are doing, swaying in time to the music.

Instead, in the middle of the dance floor, Cameron starts to do a totally bizarre set of motions that look sort of like tai chi, or some new kind of Asian martial art never before seen in the West.

Am I supposed to imitate him? Is that what a dance partner should do?

I try bending my left arm and raising my right arm to copy Cameron's pose, but no sooner do I accomplish that than he strikes a new one, with both hands clasped over his head like a genie coming in or out of a bottle.

There is no way I'm willing to do Uncorked Genie in front of half of the Southern Peaks middle school student body. People are definitely looking over at us. The couple next to us, wrapped around each other in the normal kid way, have cracked up laughing. Besides, maybe Cameron doesn't even want me to copy him. Cameron himself never copies anyone, though right this moment I desperately wish he would. He might even be irritated if I turned this into an extremely awkward version of Cameron Says. Cameron says: *Move your left hand in a long, floaty way in front of your eyes.* Cameron says: *Twirl around slowly with your eyes closed.* If he's even conscious of my existence at this moment, which seems increasingly doubtful, he probably expects me to come up with my *own* thing.

But *my* thing would have been slow-dancing with him the way every other couple except us is doing.

I have no choice but to think of *something* to do as the song continues to play. I try sort of swaying in place, shifting my weight from one foot to another and leaning first to one side, then to the other. I make myself attempt a couple of swirling motions with my arms, as if I'm waving a veil from side to side or doing a very slow version of the "Peace Like a River" and "Love Like an Ocean" motions from Vacation Bible School. Finally, after what feels like an hour but has probably only been three hideous minutes, the music ends.

I can't bring myself to thank Cameron for the "dance."

But I have to say something about his song, the song that's so beautiful, the song that sums up everything I think—I thought?—is so amazing about him as a writer and as a person.

"I love that song," I say. And I did *use* to love it. "How long did it take you to write?"

And did you write it about me?

He stares at me, utterly mystified.

"Your song," I say again. "I love your song."

Comprehension dawns on his face. "That's not my song," he says. "Hunter wrote that one."

Hunter wrote *that*?

"Oh," I say.

Just when I think my Cameron fantasies can't be any more thoroughly doused, I see Olivia slowly pulling apart from the arms of hunky Ryan. She's looking right at us, and trying not to laugh. Well, maybe I'm being overly charitable to assume she's trying not to laugh, because if that's what she's trying to do, she's failing. I can't say that she's mean to laugh, because I would have totally laughed if our positions had been reversed and she had been the one out there doing Vacation Bible School moves while Cameron was blissed out in his private Cameron world. I mean, who wouldn't?

Now that his dance trance is over, Cameron apparently notices Olivia's fit of giggles and the wide-eyed stares of half a dozen other couples who are still gazing at us. He gives a strange smile and the same slow wave he gave to Kylee and me when he saw us watching him make the rock sculpture, a wave that manages to convey total indifference to his audience, total disregard for the mirror. And yet—suddenly I see something I never saw before—it's a wave that also says, *See how cool I am that I don't even care what you think?*

So it's not that Cameron *really* doesn't care what other people think. He cares that other people *think* he doesn't care what they think. Seeming not to care about what other people think can be the biggest act of all, in its own way. And totally un-fun for the person who happens to be cast as his partner.

Which tonight would be me.

I flee from the dance floor so fast that I collide with Kylee and Tyler, who are exiting the dance floor, too, *hand in hand.*

Kylee takes one look at me.

Here's what a good friend she is.

"I have to go to the restroom," she tells Tyler as Mr. Cupertino heads back to the microphone. She gives Tyler a big, regretful smile, lets go of his hand, and half pulls, half drags me into the hall.

"What happened?"

I can't believe she doesn't know. "You didn't see?"

"No. The last I saw, you were heading off to dance with Cameron, and I was so excited and happy for you."

At least if Kylee didn't see, most likely Hunter didn't see either. Only Olivia and twenty—or thirty or forty—other people saw. But that look on Olivia's face, the look she gave me when she finally managed to stop laughing, is going to haunt me for the rest of my days: Olivia felt *sorry* for me. I felt sorry for myself.

How many dreams can one person lose?

Before we even get to the non-privacy of the overcrowded girls' room, I bury my head in Kylee's shoulder and start to cry.

26

I've been in love with part-imaginary, part-real Cameron for so long it's hard for me to know which part is which anymore.

I wonder if this happens more to writers than to other people, that we fall in love with characters we make up in our heads. It wouldn't even be so terrible to fall in love with a purely imaginary person. It's hardest if you fall in love with someone who is partly imaginary and partly real, and the real part ends up breaking your heart.

He really is a good writer. Those rock formations he made in the creek really were amazing. He really did travel all over the world. He really did write a song Hunter's band played; it just wasn't the song I thought it was. The weirdest discovery of this weird evening is that the beautiful song I loved so much was written by my own awful brother.

In a lot of ways, Real Cameron isn't all that different from Imaginary Cameron. The main difference is that Imaginary Cameron was in love with me and Real Cameron isn't. And I was in love with Imaginary Cameron, and I'm not in love with Real Cameron. But that's pretty much a total deal breaker for our romance.

"Is it okay if we leave now?" I ask Kylee, after I've told her everything. "Or do you think Tyler might ask you to dance again?"

"We can go," Kylee says.

Have I recently said that I love Kylee more than anyone in the world?

Then she adds, "Dancing with Tyler was pretty great. But I'd rather go now, anyway. I want to keep my first memory of dancing with a boy and not let anything ruin it. You know what I mean?"

Boy, do I know.

Kylee calls her parents to pick us up. My parents are out on a date night; they have a subscription to the symphony down in Denver. Mom wanted to cancel to stay home tonight to keep Hunter company—family Scrabble game, anyone?—but Dad knows how much she loves classical music, so he made her go.

"Did you girls have a good time?" Kylee's mother asks as we buckle our seat belts in the backseat.

"Yes," Kylee says, just as I say, "No."

"I have to say," Kylee's mom remarks, "that junior high dances are not my life's favorite memory. Autumn, maybe you have material for a story here?"

Kylee's mom is as supportive of my career as Kylee is.

"Maybe," I say.

But maybe not.

Usually when something bad happens to me, all I want to do is get home to write it down, to find a way to make peace with it by putting it into words with my pen.

But not this time. I don't feel like a writer anymore, and, besides, this is too embarrassing. On my deathbed, when my life flashes before me, I'll be out there on the dance floor doing weird awkward motions while Cameron is in his mystical trance, the Zen guy in the Zen zone.

I'm glad when Kylee's mom drops me off at home to an empty house with no worried mom to ask me any questions and nobody to interfere with my plans to cry myself to sleep all by my little, lonely, miserable self.

Which I do.

Something wakes me up. The digital clock next to my bed reads 11:30. It's pitch-black outside, so it's clearly still nighttime.

I hear my father's voice. He and Mom must have just gotten home from the symphony down in Denver. He's not shouting, exactly, but his voice is louder than usual, and he definitely sounds upset. Like, really upset.

The dance ended at ten, an hour after Kylee and I bailed. Was Hunter's ungrounding just meant to be long enough for him to play at the dance? Was he supposed to be home again right afterward? Is Dad yelling at him for staying out too late? Or is he yelling at Mom because Hunter's not home yet?

I try pulling my pillow over my ears. I've had all the hideousness I can take for one night. But curiosity gets the better of me, the fatal flaw of cats and (former) writers. I slip out of bed and creep to the top of the stairs in time to hear Dad race out to the garage, banging the door behind him. The big garage door whirs open. The car's engine starts.

Back in my room, I tie on my fluffy robe and scuff my feet into my bunny slippers. I'm shivering now from cold and from dread.

I find my mother in the kitchen, her head buried in her folded arms on the kitchen table.

"Mom?"

She looks up as if she doesn't recognize me.

"Oh, Autumn, honey, go back to bed."

"Is everything okay?" I ask, claiming the prize for dumbest question asked in the history of the world.

"Hunter's gone," she says.

"I know," I say, puzzled at her telling me something I obviously already know. "He was at the dance."

"The dance?" she asks, as if what I've said makes no sense. Then, as if I haven't spoken, she adds, "The Subaru's gone, too."

It all starts to sink in now.

"But . . . Hunter couldn't have taken the car. He doesn't have a license. He only has a permit, so it's against the law for him to drive without a grown-up in the car."

"I know," Mom says dully. "Believe me, I know."

So Hunter *wasn't* ungrounded for the night, reprieved from "consequences" by Dad so he could honor his commitment to play at the dance. He's AWOL and a car thief, too, though I guess the crime of taking your own parents' car doesn't count as grand larceny. But driving without a license, when you don't even *have* a license, is definitely illegal.

Plus there's the small matter that Hunter doesn't really know how to drive.

Dad's been out looking for him; Mom just called to tell

him that Hunter was last seen playing with the band at the dance. So maybe Dad's driving past David's house? Timber's? Moonbeam's? I don't know if he called their parents to ask if they've seen Hunter. Maybe they're already asleep for the night and not answering their phones.

If Dad doesn't see our Subaru parked in front of someone's house, where would he look next? I guess he's just so worried about Hunter he has to be out of the house at least doing *something*.

Mom and I are sitting at the kitchen table drinking herbal tea, not even trying to talk anymore about anything— because what is there to say?—when the phone rings. It's the landline, not Mom's cell phone, which she has right beside her mug. I can see the caller ID light up with the words "Broomville Police."

She snatches up the receiver.

"Yes, this is the Granger residence." Then: "No," she says. "Oh, no!"

There has to have been an accident. Why else would the police call our house at one in the morning?

And the last thing I ever said to my brother was that I wished he was dead.

27

Spoiler alert: Hunter's not dead—he's not even injured—but the car is totaled.

A police officer brings Hunter home in her squad car, something that would have thrilled him to pieces when he was ten but is not thrilling him one tiny bit now. I'm not in the family room when the officer comes in with him; I'm within hearing distance but out of sight in the kitchen.

It does feel like I somehow made this happen, like I have this magical wishing ability, except that it's powerful enough to get me part of what I wish for but not all of it. Like in this terrific book *Half Magic* I read as a kid, where the children find a magical coin that will grant them half, but only half, of anything they wish for. I wished Cameron would ask me to dance during "his" song, and he did, only it turned out not to be his song, and he didn't dance *with* me, just *near* me. I wished Hunter would die—well, I didn't really wish it, but I said it and at the time it felt like I was wishing it because I was so hurt and furious. And Hunter did have an accident that might have killed him, and he did totally wreck the car. Of course, none of my wishing for publication came true at all; all that wishing did was just make me give up on my writing dreams forever.

The moral is: I need to be careful what I wish for.

But I also need to be careful never again to say anything as hateful as what I said to Hunter that afternoon, because if he had died, I would have had to live with it for the rest of my days.

The officer, who introduces herself as Officer Williamson, explains to our parents—Mom called Dad, and he's home now, too—that it was a single-car accident. Hunter took a corner too fast, lost control of the car, and hit a tree. It's kind of miraculous—or *maybe* magical?—that he wasn't hurt. He has a court date where the judge will decide what will happen to him.

I can't see Hunter's face as Officer Williamson is saying all this, but I can imagine it: trying to look like he doesn't care in front of my parents, but to look like he does care in front of the police officer, in case she has to write a report that might determine his fate. She asks him some direct question I can't catch, but I hear him answer, "Yes, ma'am." So he's definitely trying to act like a kid who deserves a second chance rather than a kid who should be sent away to reform school or wherever they send incorrigible kids these days.

"I'm sorry this happened, Officer," Dad says. "I know my son is sorry, too."

"Thanks for bringing him home," Mom adds.

The officer says, "Well, we were all young once," as if all young people break the law and smash up automobiles. Then she says good night and leaves.

I can't miss out on what's going to happen next, so I take my chances and creep into the living room and do my trademark small-little-ball thing on a corner of the couch. My parents and Hunter don't even seem to notice. I've heard people say, when they can't stop looking at something, "It's like the way you can't stop looking at a car wreck." I've never had any desire to look at a car wreck. But I can't stop looking at what's happening *after* this car wreck, to my family.

"Hunter," Dad finally says, "I'm too upset to talk to you right now. As long as I live, I pray I never have to go through another night like this, wondering if my son is alive or dead. I hope that by morning you'll come up with something to say that will make us understand why on earth you thought you had a right to defy our rules, wreck our car, and break our hearts."

With that he turns and walks heavily up the stairs to bed. Dad knows how to make an exit.

Now it's just Mom and Hunter. And me, but I don't count. I'm still wearing my cloak of invisibility.

"Hunter," she says in a low, wobbly voice, "how could you?"

Hunter's ears flame scarlet. "Dad had no right to make me miss my gig just because he doesn't like my grades. I didn't even fail anything. I only got two D's. Two!"

"Of course he had a right!" Mom says. Gone is the mother who was trying to take Hunter's part yesterday, suggesting he shouldn't be "grounded," he should just "limit his activities" so he could concentrate better on school. "He's your father! He cares about you! He wants to help you make the right choices in life to give you the best chance at realizing your dreams!"

Hunter laughs then, as if what Mom said is the most hilarious thing he's ever heard.

I hear myself opening my mouth. "That's true," I chime in, like a little echoing parrot. "That's exactly what he said."

Both Mom and Hunter ignore me.

"He loves you," Mom insists.

"No, he doesn't."

"Of course he does! Just because parents have rules and try to enforce them, it doesn't mean they don't love their children. It means the exact opposite."

"Well, *I* know the things he says when he thinks I'm not listening," Hunter retorts. "And the things you say, too."

"Like what?" Mom's tone is challenging, trying to call Hunter's bluff.

"This past summer?" Hunter prompts her. "The night before school started? I came downstairs after you guys thought I was asleep, to ask you something. I forget what it was, something stupid, probably, because you both think anything I really care about is stupid."

"Hunter," Mom tries to interrupt, but he doesn't stop.

"I was still on the stairs, and I could hear you talking, and I heard what Dad said, what both of you said."

I pull in a deep breath. Whatever Hunter is going to say next, it can't be good.

"What did we say?" She looks uneasy now, as if she's trying to remember that overheard conversation and can't come up with anything but knows there might well be something he heard that she and Dad hadn't meant for him to hear.

"*You* said you hoped I'd have a better year in school this time."

"Well, that's not so terrible," I say, even though my previous comment wasn't appreciated. I so much want whatever Hunter overheard to turn out to be not as bad as he's making it out to be.

"And *Dad* said . . ." Hunter pauses, and the muscles in his jaw tighten in that exact same way Dad's do when he's upset and trying unsuccessfully to get his face back under control. "*Dad* said, 'With his dropping out of cross-country, it sure isn't looking like it so far.' And *then* he said, 'The biggest disappointment of my life has been Hunter.' "

For a moment nobody speaks. I swear, even the refrigerator stops its humming. Even the clock on the kitchen wall stops its ticking.

"Oh, Hunter, sweetie, oh, Hunter, he didn't mean it—"

"And then *you* said, 'I know.' That's what you said, Mom. You said, 'I know,' like you were agreeing with him. Like I was the biggest disappointment of your life, too."

I try one more time. I'm supposed to be good at words, though lately words haven't worked out for me the way I spent my whole life dreaming they would. But if I ever needed a reminder of how powerful words can be, this is it.

"Hunter," I say, "Mom didn't mean it that way. And Dad

didn't mean what he said either. People say things they don't really mean all the time."

Things like: *I wish you were dead.*

Mom is crying now in this wordless way, with her face all contorted and no sound coming out. I'm not crying. I want too badly to find words to say that could somehow make this be all right. But that's the thing about words. They can't ever really erase other words. They can scribble over them, but they can never make them totally go away.

Hunter juts up his chin, as if daring us to say another syllable. Then he stands and walks away, clomping up the stairs to his room, while we listen to the silence.

28

I sleep in late on Saturday. I'm stunned when I look at the clock: 11:30. Stunned both because I've never slept this late before in my life, and because it's the exact same digits I saw when I woke up to find that Hunter had disappeared. Was that really just twelve hours ago?

I'm afraid to go downstairs, but I don't have any choice. So I do.

I don't see anybody. My chest tightens. For a moment I wonder if Hunter could have stolen Dad's Jeep and run away with it in the night while the rest of us were sleeping. Maybe my parents are off desperately trying to find him.

Then I see Mom, poking her head from the garage into the kitchen, dressed in slacks and a yellow sweater, her face normal looking as if the events of last night had never happened. "Go throw some clothes on, sweetie. Your dad and Hunter are in the car. We're heading out for brunch.

We didn't want to wake you, but we'll wait for you to come with us."

Maybe I should let them go without me. Maybe they need to talk without me there.

But I'm part of this family, too.

Three minutes later, I've pulled on a pair of jeans and a ratty sweater, jerked a comb through my hair, and done the world's fastest brushing of teeth. I'm in the backseat next to Hunter, with Dad at the wheel, which is much better than being in the backseat all by myself with Hunter at the wheel.

Dad drives to this mom-and-pop breakfast place named Ya-Ya's that's usually really crowded on weekend mornings and doesn't take reservations, but for some reason today, when the hostess lady asks, "Party of four?" and Dad nods, she leads us to a booth right away.

Maybe it's a good omen. I try not to believe in omens, good or bad, but I'm grateful that we don't have to wedge ourselves into the little bench by the front door trying to think of what kind of conversation to make on the morning after Hunter wrecked the car and told our parents that he heard them say he was the biggest disappointment of their lives.

Of course, we're still going to have to talk once we settle into the booth, but maybe the talking thing will be easier in a restaurant than it would be at home. We can't shout in a restaurant. We can't get up and stomp away from the table. We can't do or say anything that would make other people look at us funny.

Our parents sit on one side; Hunter and I sit on the other. It takes everyone a while to decide what to order, except for me, because I already know I want the pumpkin pancakes. Mom finally picks eggs Benedict, and Dad picks a Denver omelet. I thought maybe Hunter would refuse to order anything, like in a Gandhi-style hunger strike, but he orders fried eggs, bacon, hash browns, and a side of pancakes. And after all, for whatever reason, he did agree to come. As far as I know, nobody had to drag him bodily to the car.

We tell the waitress our order just as if we were a normal family.

I have a strange thought: We *are* a normal family.

This *is* what normal families do. They order bacon and eggs. They say terrible things that hurt each other. They feel horrible afterward. And then they try somehow to make it better.

For a while, nobody says anything. This might be the most awkward moment of my twelve years on this earth, which is saying a lot given a certain very recent, very awkward moment with a certain boy at a certain dance. So I do what I do whenever we come to Ya-Ya's for breakfast.

I make a tower out of the jam and jelly packets, trying to see how tall I can build it before it topples over. It's interesting that it always does topple over, given that the packets are all the same size and shape and perfect for stacking. But at some point they eventually do.

My first tower topples over when I put the twelfth packet—orange marmalade—on top. My second tower topples over with the eleventh one—strawberry.

No one has yet said anything.

If somebody doesn't say something soon, I'm not going to be able to tell myself that we're a normal family having a normal breakfast.

"So," Dad says, as if we were already in the middle of a conversation and he's just throwing out a new idea for us to consider. "Sports were just—they were so important to me when I was in high school. I wanted you to have what they gave me. Being on a team. Learning to play as a team. How to win as a team, how to lose as a team. It was just . . . hard on me, knowing you weren't going to have the chance for that."

Hunter doesn't say anything.

"And, yes, I was disappointed that you weren't even going to give yourself that chance." His voice is low now. "I wanted that chance for you. I wanted it more than anything."

"A band is kind of like a team," I say, even though no one—as in *no one*—has asked me to weigh in on this.

"A band *is* like a team," Dad agrees, looking at Hunter and not me as he says it. "Maybe music is for you what sports were for me. Maybe I just couldn't see that."

"Hunter writes songs, too," I add.

Mom helps me out. "What kind of songs?"

"Good songs," I say. "The band played one at their gig a few weeks ago, and they played it again last night. It was the best song the band played."

Maybe I shouldn't have mentioned last night. Are we supposed to be pretending it didn't happen? There are limits to what even good pretenders can pretend.

"What was it about?" Mom asks Hunter.

"Nothing," Hunter growls, but it might be an okay sort of growl. He was never one for Q&A at mealtimes.

"I didn't know you were into songwriting," Dad says.

This would be a moment where Hunter might say, *Further proof that you don't know anything about me.* But he doesn't. He shrugs. It might be an okay sort of shrug.

"I've written words for some songs," I say. "But I don't know how to write music. I think it's cool that Hunter writes the music, too."

"Do you have any other gigs coming up?" Dad

asks. The word "gig" sounds strange coming out of his mouth—like when Mom talked about "pot" and "weed"—like he hopes he's using the right lingo but isn't completely sure.

"Moonbeam got us a thing at another coffee shop next weekend," Hunter says, through a big mouthful of hash browns. When he finally swallows them he says, "So . . . can I go? Or am I still grounded?"

Dad exchanges a glance with Mom. "I'd like . . . to turn over a new page. Make a fresh start. Me with you, you with me. What do you think?"

Hunter gives a grunt that sounds like an okay grunt. But then he manages a shaky grin and actually says the word "Okay." And then says the word "Thanks."

"How are your pumpkin pancakes?" Mom asks me.

"They're good," I say. They even have pumpkin syrup to go with them, which might sound like too much pumpkin but isn't. There is no such thing as too much pumpkin.

"Make sure you brush your teeth when we get home," Dad says to me. "You have to be extra careful with sticky substances now that you have your braces."

And that's how the rest of the meal goes. Dad doesn't say anything about grades or college or making sure you have choices in life, but I think Hunter knows that Dad still thinks those things matter. Maybe down deep Hunter knows that they matter. They just aren't *all* that matter.

I can't finish my pumpkin pancakes even though I adore them; I'm too full. So Hunter leans over my plate and spears a big bite, and that makes me happy. I'm even happier when he reaches over and adds a grape jelly packet to my new tower—number thirteen—and sets a Granger family jelly-stacking record.

It feels, in its own way, like a beginning.

I scrambled into my clothes so fast before heading to the restaurant that I forgot my phone, so when we get home and I turn it on, it's been hours since I checked it last.

I have a text from Kylee: **U OK?**

And I have an email from the *Denver Post*.

For a moment I can't figure out why the *Denver Post* would be writing to me.

Then I remember: the essay contest. Is it still mid-November, when they were supposed to notify the winners? Or is it time now to notify the losers?

I open the email.

It begins, "Congratulations!"

I've won first prize.

Me.

29

Standing there by my unmade bed, I feel my smile spreading ever wider, like the Cheshire Cat in *Alice in Wonderland*, who disappears and only this huge, toothy grin remains.

I read the email over and over again. There's a winner for each age, so five winners total, and I'm the winner in the twelve-year-old category. In order to accept my prize of two hundred dollars, I have to electronically sign and return a form saying that this is completely my own work and not copied from anywhere else (which of course it isn't) and that I'm giving my permission for publication (which of course I am). If I choose to decline, an alternate will receive the prize in my place. Like anyone would decline two hundred dollars and publication in the biggest newspaper in the state of Colorado!

I should call Kylee! She'll be as happy for me as I am for myself. Maybe even happier.

First, though, I find the message I sent to them with my essay attached, so I can read what I wrote over again and imagine it in print on the op-ed page for hundreds of thousands of readers to see.

I'm five, and I'm afraid of the dark.

That's a good first line. I really think it is. Even those two literary agents would have to say it was.

I read on about Mrs. Whistlepuff and the flashlight Hunter gave me. And then I read the part about how Hunter changed, and how he quit cross-country, and how my father looked at him with disgust in his eyes, the look—even though I didn't say this in my essay, because I didn't know it yet—of someone who was about to say that his son was the biggest disappointment of his life.

The girl in the essay doesn't know why her brother changed.

The girl who wrote it does.

What will Dad do when he reads it? How will Hunter feel when he reads it?

I know this sounds crazy, but somehow I never really made the connection between "getting published" and "having other people read what I've written"—not just reading my name on the byline and being impressed that I got published, but reading the published piece itself.

Other people, like my father.

Other people, like my brother.

Not imaginary readers in far-off places, but actual people I actually know.

The people I actually wrote about.

I have to talk to someone.

I text Kylee back: **I'm OK. More later. You + Tyler = Cute.**

Kylee has been the person on the whole entire earth who has believed in me most as a writer. But she's not the person I need to talk to now.

The person I need to talk to is Ms. Archer.

My parents must have a phone book. A phone book gets delivered to the doorway a couple of times a year in a plastic bag, and my mother recycles the old one and puts the new one somewhere. But where?

I find it on a shelf in the kitchen where my mom sticks all kinds of stuff she doesn't know what to do with. When I search the A's, there are a lot of Archers listed, at least twenty. I can't remember Ms. Archer's first name. But then I see Ilana Archer, and I know that's her.

Is it okay to call her at home? On a weekend? And not just any weekend, but the first weekend of Thanksgiving break? Maybe she's traveling to visit her family. I don't know if she has a family; she's never mentioned a husband. But everybody has some kind of family. Does she never mention hers in class because she doesn't think families are the kind of thing teachers should talk about?

Would she think families are the kind of thing writers should write about?

When I finally make myself dial her number, I almost hang up after two rings but I wait, and then on the third ring, someone picks up and a voice says, "Hello?"

"Ms. Archer?" I ask.

"This is she."

"It's Autumn. Granger. From your class. From your journalism class. At school."

I can't stop myself from babbling, but she says, "Autumn!" as if she's pleased to hear from me, but maybe a little perplexed, too.

"What's up?" she asks then.

"There's, well, something I want to talk to you about."

"What is it?"

I don't want to tell her on the phone. I want to tell her in person. I want to see her face when I'm doing the talking, so that I'll know what she really thinks, from seeing it in her eyes, not just hearing her voice coming through the phone. It's weird, but I want to see her long earrings dangling as she speaks. In class when she nods her head, they bob, and when she shakes her head, they sway.

"Would it be possible . . . It's the kind of thing I'd rather tell you in person. I mean, I know you're busy and all. With Thanksgiving and everything. But it can't wait till after the break."

Please please please please please please say it's all right and you can meet with me now, today, right this very minute!

"Could you meet today?" she asks.

"Yes!"

"At a coffee shop, perhaps?"

"Yes! Like, at the Spotted Cow?" It's the only coffee shop I can think of that I can ride my bike to without my parents having to drive me. "Like—now?" So I don't drop dead of a heart attack from the agony of wondering what I should do.

"The Spotted Cow in half an hour," Ms. Archer agrees.

I click off the phone, my pulse throbbing as if Hunter were beating out the rhythm of a rap number inside my head.

"I'm going for a bike ride!" I call to my mom, who is

lost in the most recent issue of *The New Yorker*, a magazine I hated until I opened the essay contest email half an hour ago. Well, maybe I still hate it a little bit.

"Wear your helmet!" she calls back, as if there has ever been a time in all my twelve years when I haven't.

Ms. Archer is there when I arrive, sitting at a table near where Kylee and I—and Cameron—sat on the night of the gig.

"What would you like?" she asks, standing up to head over to the counter to buy me a latte or a steamer. She already has her own cup of what looks like plain black coffee. She's not wearing one of her flowy skirts; she has on jeans and a dark blue sweater. But she does have long silver earrings with tiny dangling bells.

"I'm fine," I say.

All I want is to tell her what this is about.

I sit down.

"You know that contest?" I ask.

"What contest?"

"The one for the personal essays? Written by kids?"

"Of course," she says.

I hand her the email, which I printed out at home, and watch as she begins to read.

"Oh, Autumn!" She looks up at me, her face wreathed with smiles. "Congratulations! This is wonderful news! Thank you so much for sharing it with me in person!"

"Thanks," I say, wishing I could be as happy for me as she seems to be. "It's just that . . . I don't just get a prize for winning. I get published, too."

"I know! Autumn, I'm so proud of you. I think every writing teacher dreams of playing some role in her students' first publications."

"But . . . the thing I wrote. It was about my family. Well, mainly about my brother."

I'm glad I remembered to bring a copy with me. Wordlessly I hand it to her and wait as she reads it. She's already read the Mrs. Whistlepuff part before, but it's the new part that matters. She reads slowly, her face without expression. Then, when she's done, she looks up at me and I can tell from the way she tilts her head to one side that she gets it.

"What should I do?" I ask her.

Ms. Archer is the wisest person I know, and she's a published writer, so she probably deals with this kind of question all the time.

"I can't tell you that," she says.

I should have known that was what she'd say. If she

wouldn't even tell me what my Mrs. Whistlepuff essay was supposed to be about, she's not going to tell me what to do here.

I won't let her off the hook so easily.

"What would *you* do, if *you* were me?"

"Oh, Autumn, I can't tell you that either."

She insists on buying me something to drink and eat, so I order the same chocolate-raspberry-hazelnut steamer I had on the gig night, only this barista isn't as flexible as the gig-night guy, and she says she can't mix flavors. If you have to have just one flavor, it might as well be vanilla, so that's what I end up with. I don't order any of the pastries in the case, even though there are almond croissants. There's a kind of terrible stress that makes you eat three pieces of coconut cake, but there's an even more terrible kind of stress where you can't bear the thought of eating anything at all.

"A lot of people publish things about people in their own lives," I say, hoping I'll get a clue by trying out different thoughts and seeing some involuntary flash of approval or disapproval in her eyes.

"True." No flash.

"And if everyone wrote only cheerful nicey-nice things about their lives, then—I don't know—all the people who have un-nicey-nice things in their lives will feel even more lonely, like, oh, look how happy everyone else is all the time, so why am I the only one who's so miserable?"

I think back to the day in class when we talked about personal essays. I was the one who said people like to read them so that they'll feel a connection with someone else who has struggled with a hard thing in life and made it through.

I might see a tiny positive flash in Ms. Archer's eyes this time. Her earrings gleam.

"True," she says again.

"I saw this cartoon once," I say. I think I may have seen it in *The New Yorker* that day I was trying to read their nonrhyming poems. "In the cartoon, there's this author at a book signing, and her parents come up to her, and they say, 'If we had known you were going to be a writer, we would have been better parents.'"

It isn't as if I didn't give my family fair warning I was going to be—that I *am*—a writer.

Ms. Archer laughs. Does this mean she agrees that brothers have no right to complain when their sisters publish essays about them? Or just that she thinks the cartoon is funny?

"It's shallow to care about being published, right?" I ask her.

"What do you think?"

Well, whether it's shallow or not, and whether Cameron would care about it or not, I do still care about being published. And I bet a lot of other writers, throughout the history of the world, have cared about that, too.

"No," I say, answering my own question. "Or, maybe, not in a bad way?"

Ms. Archer nods this time, which I don't take as a nod of approval, more a nod of understanding what I'm saying and why I'm saying it.

It's really helping me to talk this over together, even though the conversation so far has been entirely one-sided.

"But . . ." I say.

But then there's my parents and Hunter actually *reading* this. There's the dark secret Hunter carried inside that is sort of laid out here for everybody in the world to know. It's not really my story to tell; it's Hunter's story, if he ever wants to tell it. And yet it is my story, too, because it made him change toward me, and that's what the essay is really about. When you're in a family, it's not clear where one person's story begins and another person's story ends.

"But . . ." I say again. I don't finish the sentence.

Ms. Archer doesn't finish it for me.

"But . . ." she echoes.

I swallow down the dregs of my steamer. I've gotten no clue from Ms. Archer, really. None. We get up to go.

"I have to return the form by the Sunday after Thanksgiving," I tell her. "I have to let them know either way by then."

"I hope you'll make the choice that feels right for you," Ms. Archer says.

She was nice to meet with me on a Saturday, and to buy me a steamer, and to listen as I tried my best to think this thing through. But in the end she was no help.

Neither choice feels right to me.

Both choices feel as wrong as wrong can be.

30

We're going to be spending Thanksgiving at my aunt and uncle's huge house up in the mountains, with lots and lots of relatives there; we're bringing the pies. It'll be good to have all the other relatives around to dilute our family; we're on our best behavior in front of other people. Maybe most families are.

All I can think about as I wake up on Thanksgiving morning and smell the pies baking is: *What should I do, what should I do, what should I do?*

Holidays are about traditions. In my family, for Thanksgiving we have three kinds of pie: pumpkin (of course), apple (no surprise there either), and this raisin custard pie that makes this *our* family's Thanksgiving. I always have at least a tiny slice, even though I don't like raisins when they're cooked into things, just because it wouldn't be Thanksgiving otherwise.

All I can think about as we drive up to Aunt Liz and Uncle Steve's is: *What should I do, what should I do, what should I do?*

At Aunt Liz and Uncle Steve's house, another tradition is that we all go around the table to say what we're grateful for. A lot of families have a tradition like that, I imagine. After all, the holiday is called Thanksgiving. As with the raisin custard pie, it wouldn't be *our* Thanksgiving if we didn't do this, but the tradition can also be, shall we say, a bit hard to swallow.

Uncle Steve made the rule that we can only say one thing each, because we have a couple of relatives who shall not be named who are what my father calls "pompous windbags" and would talk *forever* otherwise. And hearing a *long* list of someone else's "blessings" can make you start to hate the person just a tiny bit. So the one-thing-to-be-grateful-for rule is a good one. But picking that one thing, to say out loud in front of everybody, can be hard.

It's a total cliché to say you're grateful for your family. But if you *don't* say that, does it mean your family ranks lower on your gratitude list than the clever and interesting thing you say instead? And if you say "my health" (which I would never say, it's more what old people say), then the other old people who have cancer or shingles or arthritis might start feeling even sadder. You don't want to sound boring. You don't want to sound braggy. You don't want to sound smug. I'm telling you, it *sounds* nice to go around the table sharing blessings, but it's more dangerous than you might think.

This year, when we sit down at the huge, long table in the soaring, stone-walled great room, my little cousin Molly goes first. She's four, and she's grateful for her new puppy; my six-year-old cousin, Tobias, is grateful for the dollar the Tooth Fairy gave him for losing his first tooth. We're off to a good start.

Uncle Randall is grateful for a "terrific season" in his construction business, which translates to being grateful he made a lot of money this year. Not so good. I hope Dad doesn't say he's grateful for being named top orthodontist for the seventh year in a row.

Too soon my family's turn comes.

Mom: "For the two most wonderful kids in the world."

That's sweet, but does she really think Hunter and I are more wonderful than all the other kids in the world, not to mention all the other kids at this very table? I decide I'm being too literal.

Dad: "That we're all together once again this year."

A safe one.

Hunter: "For being alive."

For the first time I think how terrified he must have been when the Subaru careened into the tree. Not just: *Oh my God, my parents are going to find out I borrowed the car.* But: *Oh my God, I might die.*

I don't have time to process this thought, because it's my turn. I should have come prepared, given we do this every single year, but I was placing my faith in the power of inspiration. Everyone is looking at me. Uncle Steve, who has a teensy tendency toward being a control freak, has *another* rule that you can't take more than a minute to come up with your thing. For all I know, he times us on his watch.

"Autumn?" he prompts, as the seconds tick down.

"For my brother," I blurt out. "I'm grateful for Hunter."

I definitely hadn't planned to say *that*. But what if Hunter *weren't* alive? What if he had had a funeral instead of a court date? But I didn't get *too* carried away: I certainly didn't add anything like *For Hunter, who is the best brother in the world.*

Anyway, now we're on to my great-grandma, who says, "I'll echo Hunter. Every morning when I get up, the first thing I do is read the obituaries, and if my name's not there, it's a good day."

Everyone laughs.

Hunter didn't react when I said mine, and he's not looking at me now. Maybe he wasn't even listening. Very few people pay attention to things the way I do. This goes along with my tendency to overanalyze even tiny things like what I'm going to say for Uncle Steve's gratitude round-up.

Am I grateful for Hunter? Well, I'm definitely grateful he's not dead. And that he's not as mean to me as he was before. Those are two big positives in my life. But despite what I just said, I don't think Hunter is what I'm most grateful for. Even if it's wrong to love a friend more than you love your family, I love Kylee more than I love Hunter, because she's never been mean to me *ever*, and that means more than that Hunter's not *as* mean as he was before.

If I was being totally honest—and a big family holiday meal is not the time to be totally honest—what I'm most grateful for is being a writer. I love being a writer. It's what gives magic and beauty and purpose and meaning to my life. It's the biggest part of who I am. And I'm grateful that I wrote something good enough to win a contest. Maybe that's a braggy thing to say, and I wouldn't have said it out loud in front of everyone, but it's true.

If I love being a writer more than I love being Hunter's sister—and let's face it, being Hunter's sister has not been a ton of fun these past few months—does that mean I'm ready to email the form back to the contest people?

Or not?

I'm pretty sure I know what I'm going to do, but I wait until Sunday night to send the email, anyway.

I'm crying as I type it.

I'm crying even harder as I press Send.

31

For Christmas, Kylee and I are giving each other necklaces we worked on together at her house. I love knowing Kylee will have a necklace made by me and I'll have one made by her. It's the most perfect best-friend present ever.

For my dad I found a shark puppet that manages to look cuddly and friendly even as you open its mouth to display its long row of big white (perfectly straight) teeth.

For my mom, who always says she doesn't want anything, I got a book of easy knitting patterns for beginners, some yarn Kylee helped me pick out, and a handmade coupon for five knitting lessons from Kylee herself. Kylee's giving knitting lessons all the time these days. She did start a knitting club at school, with seven girls in it and one boy. (Yes, it's Tyler!)

It's hard to know what to get for Hunter. Maybe I'll get him a cool kind of tie. The band might have a fancy gig someday where they'd need to dress up. My getting him a tie for a dress-up gig would be sort of like his getting that writer mug for me, only serious instead of funny.

Hunter had his court date. Alas, I didn't get to tag along to see what a real court date is like, in case I ever need to put one in a novel. I did ask Hunter about it; we're back to talking again.

"It was boring," he told me.

"Boring?" How can a court date be boring? I would have expected it to be terrifying. The judge enters in her black robes, and all the criminals stand to face her, their knees knocking together, as she looks upon them in her august majesty—*I am the judge, great and terrible!*—before deciding who goes to prison for life and who is set free.

"It was boring," Hunter repeated. "You wait forever in this room with a bunch of other people who are waiting forever, and then they call your name, and you think something is going to happen, but all that happens is that you go to this *other* room and wait there forever, and then they call your name again, and you wait some more, and then you talk to this guy, who's not even a judge, for about two minutes. And Mom made me wear a suit to make a good impression on the judge, and hardly anyone else was wearing a suit, so I looked like I had a great big 'P' on my forehead for Pitiful."

The suit must have worked, though, because Hunter's only punishment as a kid with a first offense was having to pay the $250 court costs plus a $75 fine, and take a driving class called Alive at 25 that's going to start in January. Dad is making him earn the money to pay for it, so all of his gig money, and then some, is going to pay his debt to society. Insurance ended up covering the loss of the car, to Hunter's great relief. Dad's even letting Hunter keep on driving with his permit. I think Dad just felt so awful about what Hunter overheard and how much it ate away at him for all those months. And guess what? Hunter's first grades of the new quarter are better, too—not great, but better.

It's a Saturday afternoon, halfway through December. The band is coming over to practice in a couple of hours. Hunter is in the family room working on a new song, trying out chords on the secondhand guitar he bought himself with birthday money back in middle school.

I plop down on a corner of the couch across from him. I love being around anybody's creativity. Every spring a bunch of artists in Broomville open up their studios so people can stop by and watch them painting, sculpting, quilting. Mom and I both love going. I always feel like writing even more after smelling oil paint or wet clay.

Hunter ignores me for a while. That's okay. I'm used to being ignored. It's good for me to practice my invisibility skills. In fact, I'm so invisible that Hunter doesn't mind singing the lyrics of the song, low but audible. His voice isn't bad. Maybe it's even as good as David's.

The song, so far, goes like this:

> "The thing I want to tell you,
> The thing I don't know how to say,
> The thing you might not want to hear,
> I need to tell you anyway."

Hunter looks up then. "What do you think?" he asks me.

I do a double-take: I can't remember the last time he asked my opinion about anything. It feels good to have him act like he cares about my reaction.

"I like it," I say.

"You don't have to say that. You can tell me what you really think."

"I really do like it," I tell him, and it's true.

Hunter strums a couple more chords. "I'm good at starting songs," he says. "I'm not as good at finishing them. I'm not sure what to do with this one."

"Maybe . . . what's the thing you want to tell her, or him, or whoever it is, in the song?" I ask. "You could put that in."

"Yeah. But I want people hearing the song to be able to

245

put their own thing in. Like, maybe it's 'I love you.' Or maybe it's 'I don't love you anymore.' Or maybe it's"—he looks over at me—" 'I'm sorry.' "

Is Hunter apologizing to me? For everything that happened?

I think maybe he is.

"I wrote something about you," I tell him.

"About how horrible I am?" he jokes, in a not really joking way.

"Sort of. Well, it's about me, too, and Dad, and . . . everything."

"Can I read it?" Hunter asks.

For a moment I'm tempted to go to my room and get the copy I put in the treasure box I keep in the bottom of my closet. In the box I still have a doodle of Cameron's that he did on the back of a journalism class handout and then crumpled up and threw away. Back in October, I saved it out of the trash when he wasn't looking. It's totally weird not being in love with Cameron anymore, having him sit next to me doing his doodles and me not even caring what he's doodling and whether the doodles contain a secret code revealing his love for me. Now he's just a smart, strange guy who is a terrific writer, a terrific rock-formation maker—and a terrible dancer.

I shake my head. "Not now. Maybe someday. Now is kind of . . . soon."

"That's a good line," Hunter says. " 'Now is kind of soon.' Hey, that could go in my song."

I make up a new verse on the spot and say it out loud so Hunter can hear it:

"But now is kind of soon,
Later's kind of far away.
If I could do it all again,
I would have told you yesterday."

"Yeah!" Hunter says. "Is it okay if I use it?"

"You want to use my lines in your song?" I ask.

Hunter nods.

I nod back. It's totally okay with me.

"Were you bummed?" Hunter asks then. "When that girl in your class—Olympia? Octavia?"

"Olivia."

"When she won that big *Denver Post* writing contest, for her essay?"

I wrote the feature article about it for the *Peaks Post*, and it got picked up in the *Broomville Banner* this week. So I do have my first publication now. But it's not as big as the one Olivia got when it turned out that she was my twelve-year-old-category alternate. It's strange. I actually liked Olivia's personal essay a lot. It was about how much she dreamed of being a ballerina when she was little, and how she felt when she found out she could never be one: there's this weird way her right foot turns inward that means she can never be good at dancing. When I interviewed her, she was just so happy about winning the contest, the way I would have been, and not braggy about it at all. And—get this—she told me she had been sure the prize would go to me! I didn't tell her I got picked first. I'm never going to tell her.

"Was I bummed that I didn't win?" I echo Hunter's question. "Sort of. But I'm going to publish my poems in *The New Yorker* someday. And I'm going to write a book they'll make kids read in their high school and college English classes. And I'll get—"

"The Nobel Prize in Literature," Hunter says, finishing the sentence for me, and he doesn't sound sarcastic. He sounds like he thinks I might really do it.

He plays and sings his song—our song—again. And it sounds even better this time.

GO**FISH**

CLAUDIA MILLS

Larry Harwood

What did you want to be when you grew up?
I always wanted to be a writer. The only other thing I even considered being was president of the United States. In third grade, I made a hundred-dollar bet with Jimmy Burnett that I would be president someday, but now I'm starting to think maybe Jimmy Burnett is going to win that bet.

When did you realize you wanted to be a writer?
When I was six and my sister was five, my mother gave each of us one of those marble composition notebooks. She told me that my notebook was supposed to be my poetry book, and she told my sister that her notebook was supposed to be her journal. So I started writing poetry, and my sister started keeping a journal, and we both found out that we loved doing it.

What's your most embarrassing childhood memory?
Oh, there are so many! One day in third grade, I decided to run away from school, and I made a very public announcement to that effect. But when I got to the edge of the playground, I realized I had no place to go, so I had to come slinking back again. That memory still makes me cringe.

What was your favorite thing about being a kid?
Kids today have more organized, scheduled activities than I did, but for me, the best part of being a kid was having blissful expanses of completely empty time to spend with my sister, making up stories about the elaborate imaginary worlds we created together. I loved having so much free time, especially during the summers, just to read, play, and dream.

Did you spend more time indoors or outdoors as a kid? How about now?
As a kid I was outdoors most of the time. Even if I was just reading, I was reading in the shade under a backyard tree. Now I'm indoors much of the day. But I do adore the coziness of being inside on a blustery day, curled up on a couch under a quilt, sipping hot chocolate with a book on my lap—the book either being read or being written.

As a young person, who did you look up to most?
I mostly looked up to characters in books who were braver and stronger than I was, like Sara Crewe in *A Little Princess*, who loses her beloved father and has to live in poverty in

Miss Minchin's cold, miserable garret, but never stops acting like the princess that she feels she is inside. I also looked up to Anne of Green Gables for her spunk in breaking that slate over Gilbert Blythe's head.

What was your favorite thing about school?
It's sort of weird and nerdy to say this, but I loved almost everything about school, and during summer vacations, I'd even cross off the days until school started again. Best of all, I loved any writing assignments and being in plays. In fifth grade, I played the role of stuck-up cousin Annabelle in our classroom play of *Caddie Woodlawn*, and that was wonderful.

What was your least favorite thing about school?
Definitely PE! I was always terrible at PE. I just couldn't do any of the sports, and one time the fourth-grade teacher made the whole class stop and look over at how terribly I was doing this one exercise. I still hate her for that.

What were your hobbies as a kid? What are your hobbies now?
Well, writing, definitely, and reading and taking long walks. Hey, those are my same hobbies now. The only new hobby I've added is obsessively checking email.

What was your first job, and what was your worst job?
My first job was working in the junior clothes department at Sears. Back then, three girls worked in one department:

one to work the cash register, one to oversee the dressing room, and one to tidy up the clothes racks. I loved tidying up the clothes racks, buttoning up the dresses that needed buttoning. I loved buttoning one dress so much that I bought it, and then found that once I had it at home I had no desire to button it at all anymore. My worst job was being a waitress. I would have done all right if I could have handled just one table at a time, from drinks to salad to main course and then dessert, but my brain could not handle juggling all those different tables at once.

How did you celebrate publishing your first book?

I don't remember celebrating it. Now that I look back, I wish I had. It's a very special moment.

Where do you write your books?

I write all my books in longhand, lying on the couch, using the same clipboard-without-a-clip that I've had for thirty years, always using a white narrow-ruled pad with no margins, and always using a Pilot Razor Point fine-tipped black marker pen.

What inspired you to write *Write This Down?*

As most authors do, I draw heavily on my own life and experiences—including those of my own friends and family—to write my stories. But then I started to wonder whether I *should* be doing this, whether this is an ethical thing to do (in my other career, I'm a philosophy professor who teaches courses on ethics). Authors need to write fiercely and freely, sharing the truth of their experience as they see it. But what if what we write hurts someone we love? Is it all right to write—and publish—this anyway? I truly don't know the answer to this question, so I decided to create the fictional character of Autumn Granger, very much like my younger self, and give her this dilemma to see what she would do. (The poem Autumn writes to her crush, Cameron, in the first chapter is an actual poem I wrote to a boy when I was in seventh grade.)

Of the books you've written, which is your favorite?

I don't have a favorite. My books feel like my children; each one has such a huge piece of my heart in it. So I wouldn't want to hurt their feelings by loving one of them more than its brothers and sisters.

What challenges do you face in the writing process, and how do you overcome them?

By far the biggest challenge is learning how to accept, and even to welcome, criticism. I hate criticism and always want everybody to love my books from the very first draft. But the only way to grow as a writer, and to produce the best possible book, is to listen to what critical readers tell you, and then rewrite, rewrite, rewrite.

Which of your characters is most like you?

Each one is like me in some way, or maybe I become more like that character as I write about him or her. I think overall the two who are most like me are Dinah in the Dinah books and Lizzie in *Lizzie at Last*. Lizzie is so much like me that I even dedicated the book to myself: "For the girl I used to be."

What makes you laugh out loud?
I always laugh out loud if somebody is trying to do something in an oh-so-serious way and then something goes hideously and publicly awry. That kind of thing makes me howl.

What do you do on a rainy day?
Write and read, of course!

What's your idea of fun?
Writing and reading!

What's your favorite song?
Gosh, I have so many. I guess I'll go with "Here Comes the Sun" by the Beatles.

If you could live in any fictional world, what would it be?
I'd love to live in Deep Valley, Minnesota, the world of the Betsy-Tacy books of Maud Hart Lovelace, which were—and are—my favorite books in the world. Sometimes I get the chance to pretend I live in that world. The books were based on the author's own childhood at the turn of the last century in Mankato, Minnesota, and I have attended

several fandom conventions there where we visit the houses of the real-life Betsy and Tacy, eat the foods they ate, sing the songs they sang, and form the kinds of friendships that are at the heart of these stories.

Who is your favorite fictional character?
In addition to Betsy Ray from the Betsy-Tacy books: Anne Shirley of *Anne of Green Gables*, Sara Crewe from *A Little Princess*, and Cassandra Mortmain from *I Capture the Castle*. Oh, and all the Penderwick sisters, especially Jane and Batty.

What was your favorite book when you were a kid? Do you have a favorite book now?
It was, still is, and always will be *Betsy and Tacy Go Downtown* by Maud Hart Lovelace.

What's your favorite TV show or movie?
I don't watch much TV. My favorite movie, in recent years, is *Julie & Julia*; I loved watching both women develop as writers.

If you were stranded on a desert island, who would you want for company?
I'd be happy with pretty much anybody. In elementary school, the teachers would keep moving my desk so I'd stop talking to the person next to me, but then they found out that I would be happy talking to anyone.

If you could travel anywhere in the world, where would you go and what would you do?
I'd like to live in Paris, in a garret, and write, and be very poor, and make money by selling flowers on the street corner.

If you could travel in time, where would you go and what would you do?
I'd go back to Amherst, Massachusetts, in the 1850s, and walk by Emily Dickinson's house, and see if she would lower a little basket out the window to me with a fresh-baked muffin and a freshly written poem in it.

What's the best advice you have ever received about writing?
Brenda Ueland says, in *If You Want to Write*, that writing is supposed to be fun, and that if we allow ourselves to let it be fun, stories and poems will just keep pouring out of us. I think she's right.

Do you ever get writer's block? What do you do to get back on track?
I don't, really. My secret is to write for a short, fixed time— usually an hour—every single day. That way I never get burned out from writing, and I never get far enough away from my story that I lose my momentum.

What would you do if you ever stopped writing?
Oh, I hope I never do! But I do love reading almost as much, so I guess I'd just read, read, read. Or teach writing, which I do already and love doing.

SQUARE FISH

If you could have dinner with any person, living or dead, who would it be and what would you discuss?

That's a hard one! I think I'd be too shy and tongue-tied to talk to any of my heroes. But I'd love to be invisible in the room, eavesdropping while some of my heroes talked to each other—maybe Louisa May Alcott talking to Henry David Thoreau and Ralph Waldo Emerson in nineteenth-century New England, or all those brilliant early twentieth-century American writers like F. Scott Fitzgerald and Gertrude Stein hanging out together in Paris.

What is your favorite word?

Hmm. I'm not sure I have one particular favorite word, but I do love words. I had one period of my life when I was struck by how many fabulous words begin with "ob": obfuscate, obliterate, obdurate, obstreperous, obsolescent, obsequious—aren't those fun to say?

What advice do you wish someone had given you when you were younger?

It's okay for things not to be okay: it's okay to fail, to grieve, to hurt inside, to lose something you love, to disappoint yourself, to disappoint people you care about—not only okay, but inevitable.

What do you want readers to remember about your books?

I always try to have my main character learn some small but important truth about how to make his or her life better. While I hope this truth may resonate with readers as well, it's fine with me if they just have fun reading the story. When I think back to favorite books I read a long time ago, it tends to be some tiny trivial-but-fun detail that sticks in my head.

If you were a superhero, what would your superpower be?
Cheerfulness: the ability to remain cheerful and hopeful in the face of any calamity or impending disaster.

What part of your life brings you the most joy?
I have four things that I call my "four pillars of happiness," four things that I make sure to have in my life every single day: 1) writing, 2) reading, 3) walking, 4) being with friends. The best part is that all these four things are within my power; they are almost completely up to me.

Do you have any strange or funny habits? Did you when you were a kid?
I chew my pen or pencil as I write—I always have. Once, a few years ago, I chewed my pen so hard while I was writing that I broke my tooth and had to spend five hundred dollars at the dentist to get it fixed.

What do you consider to be your greatest accomplishment?
I'm proud that I've written over forty books while always working full-time at another demanding profession (being a university professor of philosophy).

What do you wish you could do better?
I wish I could cook. The meals at my house are horrible. I pretty much live on English muffins with butter and orange marmalade.

What would your readers be most surprised to learn about you?
My favorite food is candy, particularly seasonal candy: candy corn at Halloween, those little conversation hearts for Valentine's Day, Cadbury Creme Eggs at Easter.

Seventh-grader Sierra Shepard has always been the perfect student. When she accidentally brings a paring knife to school in her lunch, she turns it in—but instead of being rewarded, Sierra gets placed in in-school suspension and might even get *expelled*! Are the lines between good and bad not as clear as she once thought?

Keep reading for a sneak peek.

After her short meeting with Mr. Besser, who had promised he would give the ZAP idea "serious consideration," Sierra hurried to her locker to get her lunch. At Longwood Middle School, the lunch period was divided into an eating part and a recess part. Sierra had recess 5A and ate lunch 5B. So did her friends Emma Williamson, Lexi Kruger, and Celeste Vogel, which was lucky.

Sierra opened her locker, glancing at the things she had taped to the inside of her door—a picture of snow falling on the mountains that she had made in art class last semester, some goofy pictures of her and Em taken at a photo booth in the arcade at the mall, a printout of her goals for the semester, which she had made just over three weeks ago, on New Year's Day: *Speak up more in class. Read a library book every week. Don't let people push you around.* "People" meant Celeste. *Get more involved in Leadership Club.* She had done that one already, with her ZAP idea. *Don't think so much about B.* "B" meant "boys."

And "boys" meant Colin Beauvoir, who was in her accelerated language arts class, her math class, and her French class, as well as in the Octave, the elite eight-student a cappella choir that practiced Tuesday and Thursday mornings before school. Colin with the dreamy gray eyes and the slow, shy smile. Sierra loved the way his hands trembled just a little bit when he had to read aloud in class.

Sierra grabbed her insulated lunch bag and slammed her locker shut. She was definitely doing better at *Get more involved in Leadership Club* than at *Don't think so much about B.*

The noise level in the cafeteria was deafening as Sierra headed to the table by the window where her friends sat every day. She had thought Celeste wouldn't be back yet from getting her braces tightened, but there she was, her long, straight blond hair easy to see even from across the room. Tiny, smart-mouthed Lexi sat next to her; brainy, bookish Em was sitting across from them.

Sierra sat down next to Em.

"Do your braces hurt?" she asked Celeste sympathetically.

Celeste nodded. "But look." She flashed her smile; Sierra saw that Celeste's braces were now blue, the same blue as her eyes. "I got sick of pink. Pink is so last semester, don't you think?"

Sierra knew Celeste was joking, pretending to be a big authority on fashion. But Celeste definitely was a big authority on a lot of things.

"Did you talk to Besser?" Celeste asked Sierra.

"Uh-huh."

"And?"

"He said that ZAP was a great idea, and he'd give it serious consideration." Sierra felt herself beaming.

"Grownups say that when they're not going to do anything," Celeste said.

Sierra was glad to see Lexi give Celeste a withering look. All three girls were in Leadership Club with Sierra.

"Well, they do," Celeste said. "I'm just saying."

Lexi crumpled up her sandwich wrapper into a small, hard sphere and tried to toss it into the trash can, the way the boys did. She missed.

"Are you just going to leave it there?" Sierra asked.

"I'll get it when the bell rings. On my way out." As if registering Sierra's disapproval, Lexi added, "Look, it's not like it's going anywhere."

Sierra hopped up and walked the ten feet to the trash can, collected Lexi's wrapper, and disposed of it properly.

"You can't stand for a piece of litter to be on the floor for half a minute," Lexi teased when Sierra sat back down at the table.

"You shouldn't make Sierra throw away your trash for you," Celeste scolded.

"I didn't make her do anything. It's not my fault if Sierra's so anal."

Sierra knew that "anal" was a psychological term for

someone who was compulsively neat and organized, which she was—well, neat and organized, not *compulsively* neat and organized. She hated the word, though. It made her think of Luke's nickname for her.

"Aren't you going to eat your lunch?" Celeste asked Sierra.

Sierra wasn't really hungry; she was too busy mentally replaying her conversation with Mr. Besser. And, unlike the grownups of Celeste's apparent acquaintance, she knew that Mr. Besser did mean what he said.

Celeste never seemed to want to give anybody else in Leadership Club credit for having good ideas. It was one of the most annoying things about her. Sierra had become friends with Celeste mainly because they were the only two seventh-grade girls singing in the Octave; Colin was the only seventh-grade boy.

Sierra opened the Velcro flap on her lunch bag. Hungry or not, she'd better eat something, or her stomach might start rumbling in French class, right as she was sitting next to Colin.

She opened her sandwich and was about to take the first bite when she looked at it more closely. It was *ham* and cheese, not plain cheese. She must have grabbed her mother's identical lunch bag by mistake: Sierra hadn't eaten ham or pork or bacon ever since reading *Charlotte's Web* back in third grade.

"Great," she said. "I took my mother's lunch, and she took mine."

Irritated, Sierra dumped the contents of the lunch bag out onto the table. The loathsome sandwich, two oatmeal raisin cookies, an apple, and a paring knife to cut it with.

Sierra stared at the knife as if a coiled serpent had appeared from her mother's lunch bag, poised and ready to spring.

"Uh-oh," Lexi said.

"No weapons" was the biggest rule of all the rules at Longwood Middle School. No guns, not even toy guns. No knives, not even plastic knives.

For the first time since Sierra had come to the table, Em spoke up. "Just put it back in your lunch bag. It was your mother's knife, not yours. No one's seen it but us."

Lexi, who couldn't be bothered to pick up her own trash, quickly snatched the knife and stuck it back in the lunch bag, safely out of sight.

"It was just a mistake," Em said. "You took the wrong lunch. It could happen to anyone."

Celeste didn't say anything.

"No," Sierra said. "The rule says 'no knives.' Period. Not 'no knives unless you have them by mistake.' Or 'no knives except if they're not very sharp.' I'll take it over to the lunch lady, and she can put it in the kitchen or in the office, and my mom can come and get it when she picks me up after school."

Before she could change her mind, Sierra gathered up the rest of the contents of her lunch, put them back in the bag, and got up from the table. Carrying the lunch bag with the knife inside, she walked over to Sandy, the lunch lady.

She would explain everything to Sandy.

And then everything would be all right.